JJ and the Big Bend

By Chris Spicer with Catherine Lawless

Sarah GRACE PUBLISHING
Dyslexic Friendly

First published 2019 by Sarah Grace Publishing an imprint of
Malcolm Down Publishing Ltd.
www.sarahgracepublishing.co.uk

British Library Cataloguing in Publication Data
A catalogue record for this book is available from
the British Library.

ISBN 978-1-912863-02-0

Cover design by Luther Spicer
Illustration by Daniel Coleman
Internal layout by Hannah Wooler

Printed in the UK

Dedication

For Freddie, who always measures up.

Acknowledgements

I would like to thank my co-author Catherine Law-less who took my initial ideas and created an incredible storyline. My American friends, Marie Little and Dr Penny Ewbank for taking the time to read the original manuscript and offered some great suggestions, and Robert Schoeler who assisted with the baseball dream scene. Thanks to Malcolm Down and Sarah Grace who believed in this project enough to publish it. Daniel Coleman for his wonderful illustrations, Luther Spicer for the cover design, Hannah Wooler for internal layout - and finally, J. D. Walt, whose sermon on 'Measuring Up!' in 2009 first mentioned the two stories on which this book is based.

Chris Spicer 2019

Contents

CHAPTER 1:

GET SHORTY

'Hey, don't forget to take your Mama's heels, or they won't let you on, Shorty.'

'Yeah, don't slip outta the seat belt, they don't make 'em in your size.'

The whole class burst into hysterics. JJ, or to give him his full name, Josiah James Mahoney III, held his head high, refusing to show he was bothered by the taunts.

JJ had learned a long time ago never to show his feelings in front of his classmates. He had done so a few years back and was still paying the price. JJ was small for his age but what he lacked in height he made up for in courage. While others saw a small boy with brown hair and freckles, the real JJ was always up for an adventure. He was ready for any challenge that would improve his image. Coming up was the best one of all – riding the famous Big Bend Roller Coaster.

Today he had made the mistake of bragging about it in class. Everyone knew that this ride was the stuff of dreams. One minute and thirty-eight seconds of sheer adrenaline rush. His reason for telling them was in hopes of winning favor with his peers. Maybe make him appear bigger and more acceptable in their eyes. But sadly they just ridiculed him more...

JJ wished he could magic away the next few weeks. It was April and still too long to wait for the Big Bend.

The annual vacation was a well-planned family event

for the Mahoney family. Always the second week of June, every year was a different adventure. Fishing, camping, canoeing, cycling, mountain climbing, etc. But this year was different. JJ's parents had planned a vacation that would consist of visiting two of the biggest and best theme parks in the US. Beginning at Astro World in Houston, JJ and his dad were going to ride The Electric Roller Ride. However this would be nothing in comparison to the long awaited Six Flags Over Texas and the famous Big Bend ...

He stopped daydreaming now as he noticed everyone had started laughing at him again. It seemed he had to endure even more insults.

'What did one small person say to the other on a swing?' Jenny Driscol piped up.

'Dunno,' Damon Phillips shouted.

'I'll push you in a midget!'

Everyone laughed.

'I asked Mahoney to lend me 5 dollars yesterday,' Damon Phillips said to the giggling class, *'and he said, Sorry, I'm a little short.'*

With that, their laughter erupted again. JJ's hands

were clenched into tight fists. He was beginning to feel himself go but he had promised Grandpa Joe that no matter how hard it got, he would not resort to violence.

The other children could see he was close to breaking point and this just made them laugh more. They loved it when JJ completely lost his temper and started throwing things.

No one really understood what drove him to such violence, but JJ was as confused by his outbursts as they amused others.

One time he had gotten so upset that he had crashed a chair down over Damon's desk causing books, paper, pens and ink to fly off in all directions. Another time he had thrown a tray of paint at a couple of the boys who were teasing him. The paint had got into their eyes and all over their clothes and JJ's Pa had been called into the school about it. JJ knew his Pa and Grandpa had been disappointed, but they never said so.

'*What's the worst April Fool's prank ever to backfire?*' Damon asked.

'*What?*' the class shouted, already knowing the answer.

'*JJ Mahoney*' Damon shouted, collapsing with laughter.

JJ went to jump on Damon but missed. Two of the other boys grabbed his arms and held him back until he calmed down. Their teacher, Mrs Horlick, had just stepped out to get something from the teachers' lounge so missed this particular outburst.

JJ was fighting so hard to control his temper. This jab particularly hurt...

It was while giving birth to JJ that his mother had died. His birthday was the first of April, April Fool's Day, and each and every birthday JJ was tormented by his peers and his own conscience – that by giving life to him, his mother had lost her own.

He cursed his half sister now for revealing this to his class. In fairness, she had done so to try and get them to feel sorry for JJ and to stop picking on him. But unfortunately it is human nature to feed off the weak and vulnerable and that was how his class saw him.

Damon Phillips was mean and rugged and exceptionally big for his age. JJ was just the opposite, a normal boy who wished he was taller. Damon was still coming out with yet more sick jokes. On her return JJ looked to his teacher for help, but Mrs Horlick was, as usual, pretending not to hear. JJ liked her, but he wished she would sometimes interrupt the other children from their taunts. Occasionally she would look up and say:

'Now, now children, let's try to be nice to one another please.'

But most of the time JJ was left alone to be subjected to their bullying.

The oldest teacher in the school, Mrs Horlick was a sad looking figure. The younger teachers wore bright colors and bellbottom trousers. She preferred a drab gray jacket, pleated skirt and off-white high-buttoned blouse. Her flat shoes had seen better days and the large brown suede handbag with tassels, never left her side. The only colorful thing about JJ's teacher was a glass brooch that occasionally threw multicolored patterns on the classroom ceiling – a helpful distraction in an otherwise boring day. Along with her thick gold-rim glasses and long graying hair tied neatly in a bun, Mrs Horlick had few outstanding features.

JJ had bumped into Mrs Horlick once or twice at his Pa's general store. He'd noticed that while she was friendly and polite, she could however never look him in the eye.

It would be many years later, as a fully grown man,

that JJ would finally understand the reason for her lack of eye contact. She felt guilty and ashamed. Mrs Horlick could have made JJ's school life so much more bearable had she tried to intervene and help. Instead she had chosen to turn a blind eye, allowing him to be bullied throughout those influential early years.

School for JJ was a hostile environment and the jokes did not stop at the school gates. He also had to travel to and from school on the dreaded school bus. His daily ride sometimes meant putting up with a barrage of banter from his fellow passengers, all the way there, throughout the duration of the schoolday and then all the way home.

Although the driver told the rest of the kids to '*knock it off,*' they soon started up again. So the bus stop at the end of JJ's lane couldn't come soon enough.

JJ lived with his Pa, stepmom, Bernadette, and half sister, Hannah in the ancestral farmhouse that had been in the Mahoney family for generations. JJ's great grandparents had to sell off most of the land for financial reasons, when the 1930s dust storms hit Texas.

JJ's Pa was a tall man. His swept-back hair was always scruffy as he spent most of his time raking his fingers through it. With a pencil cleverly perched on the top of his ear, he was always concentrating on his store and its takings. Pa had the same colored hair as JJ but his eyes were blue and JJ had inherited his late mother's beautiful hazel eyes.

The 1920s wooden farmhouse, with its wrap-around porch, sat on a small plot of land with wooden outbuildings that included a red painted Dutch-style barn. The house was set back at the end of the dusty lane that lead to the main road. JJ and Hannah would make the long walk every weekday, twice a day, to catch the school bus. To JJ the road seemed to get longer every day and the constant chattering from Hannah drove him crazy.

Hannah Annette Mahoney was a slim and beautiful little girl with long wavy locks usually corralled with a bandana. Fond of wearing bellbottom trousers she had a kind spirit and good manners. JJ found her irritating and liked to tease her. Hannah's initials spelt H.A.M, so JJ nicknamed her 'Piglet'.

In spite of knowing what it's like to suffer the taunts of his classmates, JJ still chose to tease Hannah. Deep down he knew that he didn't really want to hurt her, but sometimes it took the focus away from his own torment and sadly he took out his anger on his poor sister.

Being the lovely kind girl that she was, Hannah seemed to have wisdom beyond her years and tried to rise above her brother's name-calling. Hannah was only too aware of what JJ was going through. She was desperate to help him, but he had sworn her to secrecy some time ago.

She had once plucked up the courage and told her mother of the bullying. BUT it had made JJ's life even harder. His stepmom had gone into the school and spoken to the Principal who had handled it badly. Everyone had found out, resulting in JJ being taunted about being a 'Mama's boy.'

Hannah was almost two years younger than JJ and the total opposite to him. Unlike JJ, she loved school and study. Getting high grades, her head was never out of a book. However in JJ's mind she had one outstanding redeeming quality in being shorter than him. He hoped she never started wearing those crazy platform shoes.

Bernadette, JJ's stepmom, was a short slim lady. Her hair was always neatly pinned into a bun. Around the house she insisted on wearing the same old flowery apron her mother wore. And whenever possible she would wear those fashionable platform shoes that gave her the height she had always craved.

Today was Friday, which meant that JJ was more able to cope with the bullying as school was out for the weekend.

Friday nights were JJ's favorite night of the week because each Friday he slept over at Grandpa Joe's house. With that in mind he wasted no time. Rushing indoors he got changed and quickly enjoyed an after-school snack with his stepmom and Hannah.

Grabbing his bike from the barn JJ rode off down the lane at breakneck speed. Trying his best to keep up with him was his faithful friend Toby. A dog with a flimsy family history, Toby was more terrier than anything else. His dirty white coat was a scruffy mess, the result of residing in the big red barn.

Toby and JJ were inseparable. What JJ lacked in human friendship, he made up for with Toby.

The two spent hours together around the farm and going off on pretend adventures. This ragamuffin dog, for which every day was a 'bad hair day', was the closest JJ had for a true friend – that is except his Grandpa.

House rules demanded that dogs stayed outside. However, Toby seemed to mysteriously find a way to break the rules every time a thunderstorm hit. Using a form of stealth that any Navy SEAL would be proud of, Toby found a way into JJ's room and hid under the bed sheets.

JJ was secretly delighted, because in recent days, this canine outsider had become more and more an insider and found any reason to escape the barn. Much to the disgust of JJ's stepmom who, since being bitten by a dog as a child, had little love for any dog, no matter how cute or cuddly.

'Hey Toby, come on boy,' JJ shouted. Toby's tail was wagging as fast as his little legs were running to keep up with his adored human.

JJ usually carried snacks and water for Toby but realized today in his haste to get to Grandpa, he had forgotten. His backpack was full of his clothes and books for his sleepover. Fortunately it wasn't too far and Grandma always had a bowl of fresh water for Toby, as well as his own bed beside JJ's.

JJ sped off down the dirt road and Toby galloped beside him. They were almost half way when JJ slowed down. His heart leapt up into his throat as he saw Damon Phillips and his older brother walking towards him. Damon was a big burly bully who looked like he was already headed for a lineman position on the football team. With his twisted square face, dark angry eyes, he walked with I-own-the-place swagger. Something he seemed to have inherited from his brother Travis. Having a horrible habit of wiping his runny nose with the back of his hand, Damon was someone you didn't want to mess with.

JJ tried to ride around them but Damon was carrying a stick and poked it through the spokes of JJ's bike, sending him flying into the hedge. Toby barked furiously and went to comfort JJ.

Damon and his brother Travis just laughed. JJ got up and started to lift his bike and check for damage, but Damon and Travis had other ideas.

'Hey, who said you could go?' Travis said, sneering.

'Yeah, sit down, Shorty,' Damon added, and pushed JJ down again.

'So, what you got in that backpack?' Travis asked.

'None of your business,' JJ replied, bravely. He knew that there was no way he could let them look inside his bag. Inside was his cherished teddy bear, which had been re-stitched and fixed so many times. He knew he would never, ever live that down. He would rather trade his bike if he had too.

Travis and Damon looked at each other, shaking their heads, and then burst out laughing.

'Oh, man are YOU gonna pay for that!' Damon said. *'So what's it gonna be? Should we let the air outta his tires or cut the brakes?'* Damon asked his brother.

'Both!' Travis said.

JJ got back up and tried picking his bike up again. This time it was Travis who shoved him hard to the ground. Toby had seen enough and ran up to Travis barking and snapping.

'Shut that mutt up before I kick it!' Travis said.

JJ desperately tried to calm Toby but it was too late. Travis kicked the poor little dog hard. Toby yelped loudly and JJ saw red.

Hurting JJ was one thing but no one hurt Toby. JJ jumped up and grabbed a piece of wood and hit Travis across the back with it. Travis fell over and Damon jumped on JJ.

There was a horrible fistfight. Travis held JJ down while Damon repeatedly punched him. Eventually, Toby had had enough and sank his teeth into Damon's ankle and the boy screamed in agony. Travis tried to kick the little dog again but Toby had learned his lesson from the last kick and ducked sideways, making Travis spin on his one leg while his other was in the air resulting in him landing flat on his back.

Damon couldn't help his brother. He was frozen to the spot in fear and, sensing it, Toby bared his teeth. JJ, seizing his opportunity, picked up his bike and rode off. Once he had put some distance between them he was able to call Toby back.

He didn't bother turning back to see if the others were following; he just peddled as fast as he could.

JJ felt his eye closing. Damon had thumped him pretty hard. He could also taste blood and his stepmom would be fuming when she saw the rips in his new clothes.

He had to get to Grandpa Joe. Grandpa Joe would help him. Grandpa Joe always had the answers.

CHAPTER 2:

SHORT CHANGED

Grandpa Joe (Josiah James Mahoney I) was a wise knowledgeable silvery haired gentle giant, and a distinguished looking Irish gentleman. Because of his farming heritage he was in great physical shape for his age. With his brown tortoiseshell glasses and his walrus-like moustache, he was the kind of elderly gentleman that put everyone at ease. Besides his unique visual appearance, Grandpa Joe was well known for his incredible storytelling ability. Even though he was now in his seventies, children and adults would love to listen to him tell stories.

Grandpa Joe was renowned for his ability to sweep

his grandchildren off their feet in an all-embracing hug of welcome. Although a little embarrassing when he insisted on exercising his grandparent right to huge hugs, this was far better than any attempt to high-five those dinner-plate-size hands or go for his vice-like handshake.

Grandpa Joe would never do anything to hurt his grandchildren. In fact, his weather-beaten hardened exterior would melt like butter in the Texan sun whenever his grandchildren stopped by. Something Grandma, in a loving way, was always moaning about:

'You're far too soft with those children. You'd never have allowed your children to do what you let them get away with!' she was always saying.

With a gentle nod of agreement Grandpa was resigned to the fact that he was a soft touch when it came to his grandchildren.

Grandma May (Winifred May Mahoney) was an observant gray-haired lady who missed nothing. Grandma May had always worked hard to give Grandpa Joe the time needed to concentrate on his writing. She dearly loved her grandchildren; however she had a horrible habit – well at least in JJ's mind – of smothering her grandchildren with kisses. The fragrance of her

old-fashioned perfume would linger almost as long as
the red lipstick marks on each of the grandchildren's
cheeks and forehead.

Grandma May was a wonderful cook. If she knew
you were coming, she would bake her special cookies,
filling the house with an aroma to die for. Also of Irish
descendants, Grandma May was scary but lovely. You
didn't mess with Grandma, but you felt as if she would
defend you to the death, if anyone dared to threaten her
grandchildren.

Because Grandpa Joe's parents had been forced to
sell off most of the land around the family farm, he
had diversified from farming to writing. Taking up
residence in a colonial-styled house with wrap-around
porch, Grandpa had his own writer's shed built in the
middle of a paddock that ran alongside the property.

Over the years Grandpa Joe had become a well-
known author with a number of bestsellers to his
name. Writing about the lives of famous American
people and major events that had shaped American
history, Grandpa's writings were much in demand.

He was an internationally known author and locally
was viewed as a renowned storyteller with almost

small-town celebrity status. His story evenings were always oversubscribed as young and old flocked to his house to hear another episode in the life of some historic figure.

Entertainment was in short supply in Willow City. No one else could hold an audience mesmerized like Grandpa Joe. His annual reciting of *'Twas the Night before Christmas* on Christmas Eve was legendary.

Local folk would gather in Grandpa's house. Candles were lit and Grandma served up her eggnog to the adults and homemade lemonade for the children. She baked her legendary pumpkin pie and everyone would listen as Grandpa Joe told the tale. His deep gravelly voice was captivating and the crackling fire and twinkling lights all added to the wonderful atmosphere before everyone set off for the midnight carol service.

With Grandpa Joe's books in such demand, he was always busy working in his shed, attempting to reach yet another pressing deadline. An eight by ten foot wooden structure fondly referred to as 'World Headquarters', Grandpa's office had windows in all four walls, a high ceiling, no electricity and little in the way of home-comforts.

This was where those world famous masterpieces

were created. Its walls were lined with bookshelves, and a small desk, on which were two old kerosene lamps. The place of honor was given to 'Old Faithful', his most treasured possession, an antique typewriter. Grandpa would spend hours tapping away at Old Faithful.

Whenever Grandpa was busy, the only gate leading to the shed remained closed, to stop any intruders gaining access.

Set in the perimeter dry stone wall, the old wooden gate with its peeling paint, parched by the hot Texan sunshine was always closed when Grandpa was working, and no one, I mean no one was allowed to disturb him, no one that is, except his grandchildren...

JJ pushed open the gate and ran up the path.

'Enter,' Grandpa shouted before the boy even knocked. JJ loved Grandpa's office; he always felt safe and calm here. He sat on the only other seat in the shed and waited for his grandpa to finish his flow. JJ could sit for hours, captivated by the different expressions which flickered across his Grandpa's face while he wrote. JJ gazed longingly at the untouchable 'Flyer' on the desk. This model of the Wright Brothers' first plane had been on Grandpa's desk since beginning his latest book. JJ smiled; daydreaming of flying high above his tormentors where Damon looked like a beetle he could just step on with a satisfying crunch.

'There, that should do it, my boy.' Grandpa finished his sentence and slapped his knees, making Toby misunderstand the gesture as an invitation to leap up onto Grandpa's knees. Grandpa and JJ burst out laughing as the little dog kept frantically trying to lick Grandpa's face.

'Get down, you little pest,' Grandpa said affectionately.

Then Grandpa Joe noticed JJ's horrific injuries but remained calm. He pushed Toby gently to the floor and got up and pulled his grandson onto his feet and into his arms.

'Now then, how about we go and get a hot chocolate and a piece of Grandma's bread and you tell me all that's been happening?'

JJ couldn't go quick enough. He adored his Grandma's bread and cakes. Grandma always baked first thing in the morning. It was part of her routine to gather her thoughts, she would say.

Grandpa Joe let JJ eat for a while and waited for him to finish his hot chocolate, or as Grandma May would call it 'a hug in a mug'. He then poured some warm water in a bowl from the kettle on the stove and took some bandaging and antiseptic cream out of the medicine cupboard. Gently Grandpa started to bathe his grandson's wounds.

'So, how about you tell me from the start?' Grandpa Joe asked affectionately. He hoped that by bathing the boy's wounds, it would help JJ describe what had happened rather than the direct face-to-face confrontations he had tried in the past.

'I fell off my bike,' JJ lied, blushing scarlet. He hated lying to his Grandpa; however, to tell the truth seemed to be even worse.

Grandpa Joe sat beside his grandson and cupped his chin up to look at him. He flinched at the pain he saw in JJ's eyes.

'*Now you listen to me, my boy. When have I ever let you down?*'

'*N.n.n.never,*' JJ stuttered.

'*And what was our deal?*' Grandpa Joe asked.

'*To trust...*' Poor JJ was devastated and couldn't finish the sentence.

'*That's right. To trust me with the truth and if I let you down by overreacting then you have every right to keep stuff from me. So how about we start again, and let that silly mutt get up on your lap, he's itching to get to you.*'

With Toby curled up safe on his lap and Grandpa Joe's big hand on his shoulder, JJ finally told him what had happened, including all the taunts throughout the day.

Grandpa squeezed JJ's shoulder and stood up and put the kettle back on the stove before speaking.

'JJ, no one can blame you for losing your temper. The way you were treated was wrong. But listen to me, my boy, they are cowards and you are givin' them the exact reaction that they want.'

'I know but I just, I dunno. I just don't see things straight and I get real hot and...' JJ was trying hard now to get the words out.

'Do you remember the ranch we saw when we went around the Loop?' Grandpa asked, changing tactics.

'I do.' JJ's eyes lit up just for a moment. He loved walking the Loop with Grandpa Joe. Willow City Loop was an awe-inspiring historic 13-mile scenic road through the picturesque rugged Texas Hill Country landscape. He would never forget the day he had sat beside his Grandpa, watching the cowboys trying to ride so many spirited horses.

'You imagine if those guys had got all wound up and lost their temper every time they were thrown to the ground. How many times was that younger guy thrown from the black stallion? That crazy creature threw him straight over the fence. Do you remember?'

'Yeah, that musta hurt.'

'Do you remember the younger guy, he freaked out and

started squealing? Horse chased him clean outta the yard and refused to let him back on. He was scared of the animal and that animal knew it. He lost its respect and trust.'

JJ smiled. The poor cowboy hadn't stood a chance. Grandpa was right.

Grandpa Joe continued reminiscing:

'Do you remember the other guy, the owner who just laughed? How he never got thrown. He said to always remain calm and keep laughing. Remember how he told us the reason he laughed was so's to calm the horse. It made his breathing calm in his belly. I will never forget how he managed to stay on, horse went berserk.'

'Yeah, he was so cool, I'd have been flat on the ground.'

'Exactly, me too. But he knew what he was doin' and that horse grew so tired of tryin' to get him off that he wore himself clean out. Do you remember him tellin' you about the way animals behave, not being so different to humans, that if we show them our fear, that they will sense it? Getting angry in a way is a last resort, losing your control.'

'Yeah, but we've been learning all about wolves and in wolf packs, you back down and you're finished,' JJ argued.

'Only if you're the pack leader or alpha male as they're

known,' his Grandpa responded. *'For the rest of the pack, which are usually part of the same blood line, you back down and you get to remain in the pack. You get protected and fed. So unless they are pretty confident that they can conquer the alpha, which is hard, then it's best to keep their heads down and learn to live beside him.'*

'But everyone wants to be an alpha,' JJ reasoned.

'Yeah, I guess we would all pretty much like to be the alpha wolf, but you know what, there's a lot we can learn and adapt from his behavior as humans. The alpha may be the strongest but it isn't just about his physical strength. He is also smart and calm. His instincts are incredible. He knows his strength. He can't go wasting all his energy on scuffles. If either his pack or he is in danger then he will fight until the death if that is what it takes, but he chooses his battles and half the time only needs a slight show of teeth to get other predators to retreat.'

JJ knew that if his Grandpa Joe were a wolf, he most definitely would be the alpha male. He remembered a time in church, when Tommy O'Neil had turned up so drunk, that he caused a scene. It had been Grandpa Joe who had been the one to step forward and evict the younger man. Tommy had tried to lash out at Grandpa Joe, but Grandpa had avoided each blow and had politely spoken to him:

'Now, now Tommy, you don't wanna go makin' a fool of yourself in front of everyone now, do you?'

Tommy had sworn and tried insulting him, however Grandpa Joe just kept calm and quietly but firmly marched the man home before returning to church. Grandpa had refused to discuss Tommy's behavior with anyone; instead, he explained that poor Tommy had a lot to deal with right now and needed their support as a community. Everyone saw Grandpa Joe as a hero from that day!

'See that's what I was doin.' I was protectin' Toby,' JJ reasoned.

'Like I said, my boy, no one can blame you for being angry but I think it's high time you and I worked out some other strategy, don't you?'

'How?' JJ asked, with a hint of desperation in his voice.

'Trust me, buddy, we will think of something and we are gonna start by learning all about wolves so I hope you bought your books with you.' Grandpa hugged his grandson again.

'Alright. I'd better get back to my Old Faithful. He 'n I have lots to finish before dinner. Grandma May shouldn't be too long, she's helping your Pa at the store.'

'Don't suppose I can come and sit with you, can I?' JJ asked. 'Only I can carry on doing my homework.'

'Sure you can and speaking of wolves, make sure you bring that mutt. He stole from the table last week! Grandma May had baked a casserole, she turned her back for a couple of minutes and he'd got up on the table and was helpin' himself to the steak and ya know Grandma will ban him if he does it again.'

The two of them laughed because they knew that Grandma May would never, EVER ban Toby; she loved the scruffy little dog as much as they did. As though he knew they were talking about him, Toby started licking JJ's face and ears, making him squirm with laughter.

CHAPTER 3:

TOWN CALLED BORING

'*Damon,*' shouted Robert.

'*Billy,*' John said.

The boys were choosing their baseball teams now. JJ stared ahead with indifference knowing what was coming next.

'*Todd,*' shouted Robbie ...

JJ had tried to take on the role of 'the competitor' but his physical size made him more often than not the team substitute. He'd love to be part of Willow's little league baseball team, but spent most of the time sitting on the bench secretly hoping to get to play, even if it was just to make up the numbers when someone else was either ill or had for some other reason not turned up. If only someone would just accept JJ as a possible player, instead of thinking of him as 'Diddly Squat', someone too short to run, catch, pitch or bat.

'OK,' Coach Cole said, clapping his hands as he did so, 'JJ, that makes you substitute; go wait on the benches. OK guys, let's get in position.'

'Too bad, Shorty!' Damon sneered and barged into poor JJ, nearly knocking him onto the ground. JJ was about to take a swing back but he remembered what Grandpa had said and managed to stop himself in the

nick of time. Instead he thought of the ranch and the cowboy's words of wisdom and smiled. He then went to sit on the bench and to daydream ...

If only he'd been born taller, richer, had more important parents. Maybe then he would have had the opportunity to fulfill his dream of becoming a major league baseball player.

Had his life been different, he would have moved to Los Angeles. There he could support the Angels, who were members of the American League. Sadly for JJ, life had dumped him into a small town off the beaten track called Willow City, with no TV. Pa refused to have one in the house, as he believed televisions sapped children of their creative energy. So, in spite of all his classmates having one, poor JJ could only listen to the game over the radio and pour over his baseball card collection.

JJ's baseball hero was a guy by the name of Albert 'Albie' Gregory Pearson, a baseball player who happened to be the shortest player in the major leagues. JJ could be the next 'Albie', he would often tell himself, if he weren't stuck here. He hated Willow and felt cheated by where he lived.

JJ shook his head and squeezed his eyes shut real tight. He always did this to calm himself down. He sometimes felt as though he was hurtling at a great speed into the unknown and he was scared.

JJ didn't like getting into trouble at school, but it just seemed to follow him. Mrs Horlick had called Bernadette and his Pa in to speak to them several times about his poor grades. Sadly for JJ, he had no idea why he got bad grades, all he knew was that he kept losing concentration. Every day he promised to try harder and yet no sooner had he sat at his desk, he lost interest.

Homework was almost impossible for poor JJ. The work set for him seldom made sense because he hadn't been listening in class.

He had recently started having strange sensations in his stomach and chest. Doc Mason had said there'd been nothing wrong and that he was just anxious. However his lack of concentration and anxiety result-ed in him receiving low school grades. This all helped to make his self-esteem spiral into a cold dark place, where he seldom felt any light.

Daydreaming and staring out of the classroom

window rather than listening to Mrs Horlick was always getting JJ into trouble. When not paying attention to her, he was often dreaming of the day when things might be different ...

'One day when I'm older,' he thought, *'I'll be big and strong enough to never have to put up with all this bullying ... then I'll get even!'*

JJ hated school and always had. When he got home after his first day he announced to his family, *'I tried school and I don't like it, so I've decided school isn't for me and I'm not going back.'* Sadly for JJ, he had learned a tough lesson that day, that children had very few rights when it came to being able to say no. His Pa could refuse to do stuff and it was acceptable, so why not for JJ? Life was so unfair.

For JJ Monday through Friday was just a countdown to that moment when life began on Friday nights at his grandparents'. He longed for school breaks where he got to spend as much time as possible with his Grandpa.

Sometimes things built up inside JJ that were like a steam engine building up steam. Certain people, objects and events seemed to fuel his fire to the point where he felt that if he didn't let off steam he was going to explode.

Without a television to distract him, JJ used his imagination to create his own form of entertainment. He could turn the barn and backyard into almost anything he dreamed up. He smiled as he remembered all the fun he had had yesterday...

He had found a pair of old steel roller skates and had managed to fix a wooden board to them to create his very own skateboard. His knees and elbows had been the painful reminder of how disastrous his first attempt at skateboarding had gone. Forever faithful, Toby had nervously trotted beside JJ and each time he had crashed to the ground, his companion had been there to lick his wounds. The last fall had been particularly disastrous!

It didn't matter how awful his day went, as soon as JJ thought of Toby or Grandpa Joe this never failed to make him smile and feel a warm glow inside.

Apart from Grandpa Joe the only other living being in whom JJ ever confided was Toby. Toby appreciated JJ no matter what. Size didn't matter to Toby. And although others might see Toby as a dog of questionable pedigree, to JJ he was the most beautiful creature in the world – a faithful friend who never failed.

JJ smiled in anticipation of Toby's enthusiastic welcome. No matter how down JJ was feeling Toby would always listen, no matter what.

The lonelier JJ became, the more isolated he felt from his family. When he couldn't be with his Grandpa, he and Toby would often hide out in the red barn's hayloft. A place JJ felt safe and secure from the horrors of the outside world.

As soon as JJ got home today, he and Toby headed straight there. One of the promises that JJ made to Grandpa Joe last Friday was to write his feelings down. Grandpa had even given him his very own book and pen, which JJ had safely hidden in the straw.

JJ had been pleasantly surprised by how many words he had managed to write each day in his journal and Grandpa Joe had been right about one thing, writing it down did make him calmer somehow. Grandpa had explained that *'writing it down, takes it out of your head and helps to make sense of it all ...'*

SATURDAY.

Me and Grandpa Joe took Toby around the Loop.
Toby dived in Coal Creek and Grandpa Joe had to
get the silly mutt out. Grandma May pakked us
the best picnic so me and Grandpa and Toby sat
while he dried off in the sun. I wish I could
live with Grandpa Joe. I hate my home.

SUNDAY

This house stinks. I hate it. This is the worst
house ever. Its freesing in the winter and
boiling in the summer. No wonder no one wants to
come here.

MONDAY

Willow City. CITY! Who in their right mind
would call this dump a city. Grandma May said
that there's only 95 adults who live here but
it's growing. How's it ever gonna grow? Who
would want to come here? If I ever get to
be Mare of Willow then I'm gonna rename it
'Boring'. That way the church would be known
as 'The Boring Bapptist Church' and school
renamed as, 'Boring School' and then Pa's store
would be known as 'The Boring Genral Store'.

TUESDAY

Grandpa Joe came by with his thing he wrote for the Willow Weekly. He is so clever. He can make the most rubish, boring news funny. He showed us. 'A farmers hen got killed last week crossing the road, and the big question is possibly, "Why did the chicken cross the road?" He said Grandma May found it funny. Pa and Bernadette didn't laugh, but they don't ever laugh and Piglet just laughs for the heck of it. I wantid to go home and stay with Grandpa Joe but Pa said not on a school night. Don't see what diffrinse it makes. At least I don't have to ride on the school bus from Grandpa's.

WEDNESDAY

Henry just had a color TV put in his bedroom. Me and Toby hid in the bush outside and I got to see sum of the game. Why can't we have a TV?

THURSDAY

One more sleep and I'm at Grandpa Joe's. They said I can stay until Sunday this week.

JJ woke up the next morning feeling optimistic. The weekend was approaching! He and Hannah made the long walk down to the end of the road to wait for the bus. As it pulled up Toby noticed that it wasn't their usual driver but was Damon's Pa instead. Mr Phillips covered whenever the regular driver had a holiday or was sick.

JJ's heart sank. He knew that he was in for trouble as Damon's Pa was as cruel as his sons. He seemed to love hearing all the other kids tease JJ until he lost his temper. He could sense Hannah scratching uncomfortably beside him.

'It may not be so bad, JJ. Just ignore them,' Hannah said sweetly.

'Yeah, right,' JJ said, putting his head down.

The bus pulled up and Mr Phillips had a horrible smirk on his face. JJ wondered if Damon and his brother had told him about last Friday's fight and learnt immediately that they had.

Hannah climbed on and JJ was on the bottom step when Mr Phillips got out from behind the wheel and bent so low that he came right up to JJ's face.

'You'd better keep that maniac mutt on a leash, "Shorty" or something really horrible will happen to him!'

The bus all roared with laughter and JJ flinched at the disgusting smell that was coming out of Mr Phillips' mouth, with its huge yellow crooked teeth. It was a mix of smoke and dead fish guts.

'So, what do you have to say for yourself, boy? Or are you gonna cry like a little girl?'

Again everyone laughed, except Hannah of course who made the mistake of getting up and trying to reach out for JJ's hand. This just made everyone laugh all the more.

JJ could feel his head getting all hot. The voices were fading into the distance and his eyesight was going all blurry. He could feel his fists scrunching up. So he did what he promised Grandpa Joe he would do. He closed his eyes and pictured his Grandpa ...

'I can't always be there with you, buddy, but just imagine I'm right by your side,' he could hear his Grandpa say.

With that JJ smiled. He unclenched his fists and stepped off the bus and walked back down the lane.

'You need to get back here now, Shorty,' Mr Phillips was shouting but JJ ignored him and made the long trek back to the house. He could hear all the other kids cheering and laughing but he didn't care and was proud of himself. He knew that Bernadette would be going to the store soon to help his Pa so he would just need to hide out in the barn until she went. She always left the porch door open. BUT not today!

JJ and Toby huddled in his den in the hayloft, getting hotter by the minute. He was beginning to get quite tearful by the time he heard Grandpa's truck coming up the dirt road.

Grandpa had guessed where he was and come straight to the barn.

'Come on, Josiah, get in the truck,' he shouted.

JJ and Toby climbed into the truck as Grandpa fired her up. JJ expected Grandpa to be cross, however he just chatted about baseball and Toby.

As they approached the school, JJ was surprised as Grandpa drove straight past and on to his place.

Grandma May was in the kitchen. JJ could tell she was finding it hard not to tell him off for ditching school. She didn't hug him either, which for Grandma May was out of character.

Grandma had set three places for lunch and told him to go and wash his hands.

The three of them dug into her delicious meatloaf and Toby was curled up in his little bed with a cattle bone. The atmosphere was a little strained; however, good old Grandpa Joe kept trying to jolly everyone along.

After lunch Grandma announced that she was going to the church to do the flowers for the wedding tomorrow so Grandpa said he and JJ would wash the dishes.

'Do you wanna let me know what happened?' Grandpa asked while washing up. He had handed JJ a towel to dry with.

'I did what you said. I walked away,' JJ announced proudly.

Grandpa Joe closed his eyes, cursing himself for a minute.

'JJ, you still have to go to school. I didn't mean walk away from school.'

'It was gonna be real bad, Damon's Pa was there and said he would hurt Toby. I could feel myself getting into one of my mood things so I turned around and walked home.'

Poor, poor little guy, Grandpa thought. He reflected on how trapped children sometimes felt. How they were at the mercy of others. How they should be protected and yet they could be trapped for years within hostile environments.

He knew that JJ struggled with understanding some things and it broke his heart that even adults were bullying the poor boy now.

Grandpa had managed to get lots done this week so it could free him some time to spend with JJ this weekend.

He had arranged to take JJ along to the ranch again. Distracted by watching the cowboys, JJ often let his guard down and revealed his feelings to Grandpa Joe.

JJ's Pa turned up all red–faced and angry. The school had sent the truant officer into the store first thing. He told him that JJ had refused to get on the school bus but Pa hadn't been able to shut the store until Bernadette showed up. Having had a few hours to dwell on it, he was furious. He marched into the house and stormed straight up to JJ, demanding he explain himself. Grandpa told JJ to go outside so that he could speak to his Pa.

'Son, JJ is in trouble and we need to help him,' Grandpa Joe said.

'He's always in trouble and I'm sick of it,' Pa argued.

'And what good is that gonna do? Unless we help him, things are gonna get a whole lot worse. Sit down, let's talk,' Grandpa pleaded.

'I haven't got time, I'm gonna have to do the deliveries and I'm already running late,' Pa said. Grandpa felt sorry for his son, he looked exhausted.

'Look, we can talk about it later. Go make your peace with the boy. NOW!' JJ's Pa was shocked, as his father never

raised his voice, so he did as he was told.

Poor JJ looked sheepish and couldn't look into his Pa's eyes. He expected a lecture or at least being grounded but he was pleasantly surprised because all his Pa did was say he would see him later.

Bewildered, but relieved, JJ went back to being Superman. Superman had just taken all the children from Willow School and flown them all to Idaho and left them there. By the time JJ was due to get to school the next day, the only one left would be Hannah.

'Oh, if only!' JJ yearned.

CHAPTER 4:

PITCHING TO WIN

Although JJ was unable to break out of the boring town of Willow, he could dream, and dream he did! He had a vivid imagination that enabled him to escape the humdrum of everyday life; however, it often got him into big trouble. Rather than paying attention to Mrs Horlick, JJ would often be found staring into space.

Although the attendance roster proved that JJ was physically present, his mind was elsewhere.

Mrs Horlick began to explain some mathematical problem on the chalkboard but JJ was drifting off. In his mind he was wearing the uniform of the California Angels and about to leave the dugout to step up to the home plate.

It's the bottom of the ninth and the Angels have two outs and are behind by three runs as JJ steps up to home plate. The fans wait to see what the shortest player in the big leagues will do next.

Fearing the worst, JJ readies himself to face the Cardinals' formidable pitcher. Having swung and missed twice, this is his last chance to either strike out, or get a hit. For those listening on the radio, the announcer describes what JJ and his team faces.

JJ could hear the words of the excited commentator saying: *'Well, here we are, fans, in the bottom of the ninth inning of the seventh game of this classic World Series between these two giant combatants: the Angels of the American League and the St Louis Cardinals representing the National League. With the bases loaded, it appears that everything is riding on*

*what JJ can do batting against ace Cardinals' pitcher,
Bob Gibson, with two outs, and a three-ball, two-strike
count. All the marbles are riding on this next pitch. It's
like watching in slow motion. JJ swings and lofts a long
high drive to deep right field that is going! Going! Gone!!
Gone! For an unbelievable World Series grand slam
home run that wins the series for the Angels!*

*Unbelievable! One for the ages that will be talked about
to generations not yet born! Wow, double wow!'*

In JJ's mind he could hear the crowd shouting his
name, but then he awoke to the fact that it was not the
crowds but his teacher shouting, *Josiah, Josiah Mahoney'.*
Having now realized that he was in a classroom, rather
than the ballpark, he heard those dreaded words,
'Perhaps you would like to tell us the answer?'

'The answer,' he thought, 'I didn't even hear the
question!' But he vaguely remembered that the class had
been given a multiplication problem to solve. To simply
offer any answer would be pointless. The normally kind
soft-spoken teacher was clearly having a bad day, and the
daydreaming, sheepish ten year old was not helping.

JJ mystified Mrs Horlick. Having taught children for
27 years, she had never come across anyone so complex

as Josiah James Mahoney. His whole visible attitude spoke of his dislike for school. While others skipped around and enjoyed the breaks, JJ, with hands in his pockets, shuffled around the schoolyard despondently. With a long face and his shoulders drooped, this was a signal to all who observed him that JJ was not a happy child.

She was astounded by his ability in English. He seemed to have inherited his grandfather's skills at storytelling. He had a wonderful vivid imagination. However, she knew that his confidence was dented severely by the other children's taunts, which prevented the boy from improving his skills and reading any of his stories out loud in class. She had tried to push him into reading once. However he had lost his temper quite dramatically so she had learned to leave him alone after that. That was another thing that shocked Mrs Horlick; JJ's temper, which presented itself when the boy was particularly upset. It was a red–hot fury that was frightening to witness.

After lunch JJ began to get that bad feeling in his stomach. He knew something awful was going to happen but he couldn't place it for a while. Eventually reality dawned ... he checked his bag several times but realized that he had left his journal at home and he didn't want anyone to read it. And once more, he'd forgotten to hide it under the straw in the hayloft.

He was still writing his feelings down, and what had started out as a couple of sentences a day had morphed into so much more. JJ was shocked by some of the things he was writing down and always tried desperately to hide his journal but today he knew he hadn't ... HE'D LEFT IT ON HIS BED!

Bernadette Mahoney sat on his bed with tears streaming down her face. Poor, poor JJ. She had no idea he was so unhappy. She hadn't meant to pry but the book had been open and her name had been written with the word *'hate'* written boldly beside it. She wished she could unread what she had just read.

Dear Mama I wish you didn't die. I HATE Pa and I HATE Bernadette. She thinks she can be my Mama but she will never be you. If you hadn't died I know you would have never made us stay in this rotten city. Pa said you liked to travvel. Me and you could have travvelled together. Pa stays here because of Bernadette and Hannah. Hannah is there anoying daughter. She was born after you died and Pa marryd Bernadette. They tell me to call her my sister but I don't. They like her a lot but I don't. Grandpa Joe and Grandma May love her too and so does Toby, but Toby likes anyone so he doesn't count. Grandpa Joe always tells me storys about you but Pa pretends you were never here and I HATE him for that and I know its because of HER, Bernadette. Damon said you died instead of me and it was Pa's fault. He said that Pa had to choose which one of us to live. Damon said everybody knew Pa chose me instead of you 'cuz he got mar-ryd so soon to Bernadette. I asked Pa but he said that there was no choice and that there was nothing anybody could do, that you just died. I know Pa doesn't love me like he loves Hannah, so maybe Damon was right. Damon said it was his Pa that told him. I wanna live with Grandma May and Grandpa Joe but Pa won't let me. I love their house Mama, its always cosy and bright and Grandma May lights candles but this place is so dingy and dark. Anyway Mama, Grandpa Joe told me to write to you because I told him I am sad when I think about you. I get these dizzy spells and go bad and angry and he said to write to you and tell you that I miss you, but its hard and it makes me feel really bad because I never knew you so how can I miss you, but I do. Anyway Mama, I guess I will be going. I gotta go to school tomorrow and I HATE it. I HATE livin' here Mama. Sleep well now Mama.

Bernadette put the journal back where she found it. She didn't want JJ to know she had read it. However, the fact that he had left it open made her wonder if perhaps he had wanted her to see it. Either way Bernadette knew that things would never be the same between them again. She felt ashamed of herself for not seeing what was going on right under her own nose.

Bernadette decided that she needed to speak to her husband so she set off to the store. JJ's favorite meal was Grandma May's meatloaf so when she saw her at the store, Bernadette asked for the recipe and she also asked Grandma May if she and Grandpa Joe would come to dinner. Grandma could see that it was a plea rather than an invitation and said of course they would, and that she would bring a homemade cherry cobbler. On hearing the invite JJ's Pa raised his eyebrows, as his wife never did anything spontaneous.

Bernadette waited until the general store was closed for lunch before revealing to her husband what she had read. At first he had been angry and apologetic that JJ could be so horrible about her, but Bernadette was a kind generous woman.

'Josiah, please stop this and sit yourself down. JJ has been carrying all this around with him for all these years.'

'You are good to him, though, Bernadette. Anyway, he didn't even know his mother,' Pa tried reasoning.

'Exactly, and how awful is that? Think about it, Martha died giving birth to JJ. If she hadn't given birth to him, she may still be alive. Can you honestly imagine what that is doing to him? It must have been eating him up for years.'

Pa sat down and put his face in his hands. By the time he looked up Bernadette could see tears pooling in his eyes. Bernadette had never seen him cry before.

'It was too soon for him ... with us, I guess. But Bernadette,

I won't say that I'm sorry. I was so lonely and I fell in love with you. I was trying to raise a three-month-old boy and didn't have a clue. Mama was great and Papa, but you saw the state we were in, Bernadette.' He was pacing now, raking his fingers through his hair, desperately trying to justify himself. He looked terrible.

'Listen, sweetie! Let's not make this about us. We can't change the past. As your Papa always says, "What's done is done". But we can make a fresh start. Let's try to see what we can do to help him. Let's have a family meal tonight and maybe it wouldn't be a bad thing to let the boy stay at his grandfolks a little more often,' Bernadette reasoned.

'He stays there every Friday as it is!' Pa argued.

'Yes but maybe the occasional Saturday too won't hurt. He loves it there and I know your Papa is really trying to help him. Hannah said that he is helping him deal with his temper.'

'Well, someone needs to do something. He's too hot headed and I am tired of getting complaints from school,' he said.

'But it isn't his fault! He's being bullied. Hannah said the kids are horrible to him.'

'Look, I need to open. Let's talk about it later. Can you cover me while I do the orders?' Pa asked.

'No, not today, I'm gonna get back and start this meatloaf. I want tonight to be special. We can't let this go any longer, we both need to wake up and face our responsibilities for JJ. We're the grown ups here. We owe it to him to try and make things better.'

Pa was shocked. Bernadette had never said no to him before. She was such a kind-spirited lady. No, she wasn't the beauty that Martha had been but she was solid and kind and had proved herself yet again by worrying about JJ. Pa closed his eyes for a second and offered up a frantic prayer for help.

The evening was a huge success. Bernadette had lit candles and the fire, sending a beautiful warm glow around the room. It wasn't really cold enough for a fire, however she had been determined to create the sort of atmosphere that you always expected at Grandma May's.

The meatloaf was delicious, as was Grandma May's cobbler. The six of them sat round and chatted for almost three hours. JJ was surprised at how funny his Pa and Bernadette were being. They smiled and laughed a lot. He like it! He'd also been surprised to see two old photos of his Mama. One was of her on a swing, laughing,

her beautiful dark hair flowing behind, and the other was of her pregnant; she had looked so happy. JJ hadn't asked why they were there but he liked it and he didn't know how he knew but he knew it was Bernadette who had got them from the old wooden chest in the attic and put them there.

Usually JJ and Hannah did the dishes but tonight Bernadette insisted that she do them with Hannah so that JJ could spend some time with his Pa and grandparents, but Grandma May insisted on being with the girls and helping.

JJ loved the novelty of being with his Pa and Grandpa. It wasn't all talk about the general store or boring things. Tonight, they bounced off each other, teasing each other and reminiscing about years gone by. JJ savored every last morsel of information, storing it safely inside his brain for when he needed some happy thoughts. Some weeks, all he got were unhappy thoughts so these were precious gifts to keep safe.

Bernadette, May and Hannah returned to the dining room with a large pot of coffee and homemade lemonade. This was where Bernadette surprised him the most.

*'So, Josiah, I was just asking your Mama about yours and
Martha's wedding day. You never told me anything about
it and I'd love to hear, and I'm sure JJ would too, right?'* she
asked and smiled at JJ.

'Sure,' said JJ smiling at her shyly.

Bernadette had already briefed JJ's Pa that they were
all to talk about Martha. She explained that not talking
about her wasn't protecting JJ like they had first thought,
but instead was making the boy unhappy. Pa had already
practiced and now described the entire wedding day from
start to end. Grandpa Joe and Grandma May, who had
also been in on the secret, kept adding their own accounts
too. It was magical hearing all about the special day.
JJ realized that maybe he had misjudged his Pa and
Bernadette. It was clear as day that his Pa had loved his
Mama, and Bernadette was enjoying listening to the
memories.

By the time JJ went to bed he was exhausted but
content. He knew that Bernadette had read his journal.
Knowing she had, had worried him earlier but not now.
She could have told him off for being horrible about her
but she didn't. She told him tonight that they all needed to
work together to help JJ cope with his feelings. She also

told him that she loved him and although he hadn't said it back, it had made him smile and feel a warm glow. Even Piglet hadn't annoyed him too much tonight.

'Maybe Grandpa Joe's right about the writing thing, maybe it really can make things change,' JJ thought, and then surprised himself by falling asleep as soon as his head hit the pillow.

CHAPTER 5:

CUSTER'S LAST STAND

The weekend came at last. Surprisingly Pa turned up for lunch on Saturday and came with some of JJ's favorite comics.

JJ lost himself in his comics. They provided him with the ultimate escape.

Captain America, Batman, Superman, Spiderman were the heroes of JJ's week, and one of the best parts of sleeping at Grandpa and Grandma's house. To learn the secret of saving the universe, the colorful animations of the comic book were a much better way of spending his time than reading those boring books Mrs Horlick asked him to read. In JJ's mind, be it fact or fiction, all lessons should come in the form of pen and ink drawings. English, Math, Geography, History or Science, all education should use animation.

Of all the books he possessed, JJ's favorite was a seventh birthday present from Grandpa Joe called, *The Battle of the Little Big Horn: Custer's Last Stand.*

Fascinated by this famous battle, JJ imagined himself as General Custer. Did Custer refuse to obey his orders and wait for reinforcements, even though the Sioux and Cheyenne outnumbered him as he fought this historic battle near the Little Big Horn River in Montana? JJ would spend hours pouring over the large-format drawings in search of the magnificent truth. The few words explaining what happened on 25th June 1876 were hardly worthy of his hero. Damon had said that Custer was stupid; however, JJ disagreed and believed that only a true hero would battle on against the enemy when he was so outnumbered.

The evenings were growing warmer and Grandma May had started to light the old oil lanterns on the front porch. This was JJ's favorite place as the three of them would sit under the stars, listening to Grandpa Joe talking about his latest stories. Sometimes, if it grew chilly,

Grandma would bring out blankets for her and JJ and they would both sit either side of Grandpa and snuggle up on the swing bench. It was here that JJ often fell asleep and Grandpa would carry him to bed.

The boy was always so relaxed here that if he did wake up briefly, it wasn't long before he would fall back to sleep, with Toby curled up in his bed beside him.

No sooner had JJ opened his eyes on a gorgeous Sunday morning than his magnificent mutt was all over him. Licking all around his ears and neck. It tickled like crazy, making the boy squeal with delight.

JJ was excited because Grandpa Joe said he had planned a surprise for him. He got up, got cleaned up, and then went down to breakfast.

Grandma May had been up early making their packed lunches. She'd also baked some bread and made scrambled eggs for breakfast. The three of them sat on the veranda eating and Toby eventually appeared, half way through. Used to the basic standards of the barn, the little dog made every last moment count when staying here. Only when his salivary glands could cope no longer, would Toby follow the delicious smells beckoning him from downstairs.

After breakfast Grandpa announced that they had
to go but that Toby would need to stay with Grandma.
Poor Toby. Being put on the long leash that was
attached to the porch was not his idea of fun. JJ was
shocked, since Toby was his constant companion
whenever they stayed at his grandparents' house.

It was a little while later that Grandpa Joe pulled his
truck off the Loop and onto the long drive leading to the
ranch. The cowboy who he recognized as
the owner came and shook hands.

'Hey Joe, so this is JJ, right?'

'JJ, I'm Jackson,' the man said
as he put out his hand to shake
JJ's. He felt very grown
up to be shaking the
ranch owner's large
thick-skinned
overworked hand.
Jackson was a
tall strong hand-
some man who
spoke with a slow
southern drawl.
His thick mane of

hair flopped to one side like one of his beloved horses. He had a habit of stroking his scruffy sideburns that protruded from his large brimmed hat, while his piercing perceptive blue eyes accurately sized you up. JJ was captivated.

'So, your Grandpa here tells me you've been showin' an interest in horses, is that right?' the cowboy asked.

'Um, yeah.' But realizing that sounded disrespect-ful he added, *'sir'* to the end, making the whole thing sound funny and JJ blush with embarrassment.

'OK, I got just the horse that could use someone to spend time with her. She's old and bored and needs a job to do,' Jackson explained.

JJ could feel the little bubbles of excitement tickling his stomach. It felt very different to the sensations that he associated with a temper tantrum. These were nice but nerve wracking.

'I never rode a horse, sir,' JJ explained.

'Don't matter, she's a good old gal so she will take care of you,' Jackson explained. *'Besides, it'll be a few weeks before you'll get up on her. You need to get to know her first, take care of her 'n all.'*

JJ felt himself relax. Much as he was desperate to get on and ride a horse, he was terrified he would fall off and mess up, like he did with most things.

'So, first we're gonna give her a good groomin' to get her nerve endings going and after, how about you spend a little time clearing her stable?' Jackson asked.

Grandpa Joe joined them for the short walk to the stables. He smiled fondly at his grandson who he noticed was battling like crazy to contain his excitement. It was written all over his face. Grandpa had brought along his notebook. He never wasted any opportunity to make detailed notes. He never knew where his writing would take him next, so decided he would sketch out a rough idea of life as a ranch hand.

Jackson walked up to a stable and a beautiful head peeked over and nuzzled him. Jackson gave her a piece of carrot and then handed JJ a piece.

'JJ, this is 'Scarlett O'Hara'. Here, hold your hand real flat and let her take the carrot.'

Poor JJ was so scared of getting bitten that he dropped the carrot several times. A furious Scarlett O'Hara was stomping her hoof in protest. Eventually after several attempts the mare finally got her carrot and turned her back in a huff.

'Stroppy old mare,' Jackson said affectionately.

'So, JJ, how about you and me get this old gal out? I'll show you how to brush her and then we can clean out her stall and let her stretch her old legs. After that, I could use a hand feeding some of the other horses on the ranch, but we will need the truck for that 'cuz they're over yonder.'

'Yes, sir,' JJ said, standing up as high as he possibly could.

JJ looked shy but Grandpa knew he was in safe hands. Jackson Lain was renowned for his patience and he had made a deal with Grandpa Joe, that he would teach JJ to ride and care for horses, if Grandpa Joe agreed to help Jackson's daughter, who was struggling with her English.

Jackson made eye contact with Grandpa Joe and their silent gesture sealed the next part of JJ's journey.

Joe had told him a little about JJ, and Jackson felt that time working hard on a ranch and spending time with the guys could only be a good thing for any ten-year-old boy, particularly one who felt he didn't fit in. A couple of ranch hands had returned from war, traumatized by their experience, and Jackson had witnessed first hand the healing power of horses, slowly and steadily building up the trust and faith of these broken men.

Jackson and JJ got to work and Grandpa Joe left them to it. JJ asked Jackson a million questions and was fascinated by the older man. Before they went to take feed to the other horses, they led Scarlett O'Hara out to a small pasture so she could stretch her legs. JJ laughed, as there was another horse in the pasture. It was the size of a mountain. Scarlett O'Hara looked tiny by comparison. But as soon as she entered the paddock and was unhooked from the leading rein, she immediately took control of the enormous but younger horse. Jackson looked sideways to JJ and smiled.

'Woah, she's really small next to him, sir. How come he don't take charge?' JJ asked, captivated by the whole scene.

'See, it isn't about size when it comes to being the boss. That old mare has been in charge since my Ma was alive, no one can tell her what to do. I've learned a lot by watching these horses, ya know. Animals don't struggle with their feelings like humans do. They rely on their instincts, 'n I guess since man has taken them captive, they rely on us to care for them. And I told you to call me Jackson,' he said, smiling affectionately at the boy.

'Sir ... I mean Jackson.' Poor JJ always stuttered when he was nervous or embarrassed.

Jackson smiled at the boy and started to walk back to the stables.

JJ thought Jackson looked like a movie star. He was a tall strong handsome man who you wouldn't want to upset. But there was a kindness and patience about the man, which reminded JJ of his Grandpa.

Grandpa Joe couldn't get over the difference in his grandson by the time he and Jackson had finished. His eyes looked alive, his cheeks were full of color and

he had never known JJ chat to anybody like he was to Jackson. His instincts had been correct and he smiled as he thought of the weeks ahead and how Jackson and Scarlett O'Hara could only help the boy gain more confidence.

Jackson got JJ to lead Scarlett O'Hara back to her stable and top up her trough with fresh water and feed. The boy had been so frightened of the horse at the start, and yet already he was relaxing around her.

She gently nuzzled JJ as though to kiss him goodbye and he turned round, desperate to hide his tears. Jackson and Grandpa Joe spotted it but pretended not to and walked on ahead.

JJ was utterly exhausted and his whole body seemed to be aching. He hadn't worked so hard in his entire life but although every muscle in his body was sore, it was a good pain, which made him feel proud of himself.

He did not stop talking all the way home and Grandpa reminded himself again that this was going to help JJ so much. The family had been talking about their concerns for JJ and how they needed to help him.

Grandpa's biggest concern was the way JJ saw himself. He knew that JJ struggled to take responsibility for his own behavior and he also knew that JJ always felt picked on. Grandpa understood how difficult it must be for a ten-year-old boy who had no friends or support at school. School was a nightmare for bullied kids. It wasn't as though JJ could escape through sports either. They insisted on allowing the kids to pick their own teams. So JJ was always a substitute who sat out on the bench.

JJ was either excluded or bullied and Grandpa Joe knew that they all needed to do something to turn it around!

JJ soaked in Grandma's tub. Somehow his Pa had agreed that JJ could stay here tonight and then go into school tomorrow. He felt relieved as he bathed his aching muscles. He smiled as he replayed the day in his mind. Already he couldn't wait to go back next week. Jackson had promised him that he could, but had also made him aware that the ranch depended on everything running smoothly. If one of the horses or cattle were sick then Jackson's time would be needed to focus on them. It was clear that, like his Grandpa, Jackson didn't like letting people down either, so prepared JJ in advance.

JJ was delighted that he could stay here another night. He was even more relieved since it meant he wouldn't need to face the school bus – which at least bought him a little time before the taunts started up. He got out the tub and got his pajamas on. Grandma May called him down for his milk and cookies. Before he left his bedroom, he picked up *The Battle of the Little Big Horn: Custer's Last Stand* again to read later. 'Least Custer had reinforcements,' he thought bitterly.

Poor JJ was facing so many challenges. Surrounded by hostiles he longed for the day when reinforcements would appear on the horizon to save him. In his mind he could hear the bugle blowing. But although help was about to arrive it would not come in the way he expected.

CHAPTER 6:

WHEELCHAIR WHEELIES

JJ took a huge breath and counted to ten, something Jackson had told him he did before getting on a new horse. He walked through the school's main door and was immediately told to report to the Principal's office. His heart sank to his shoes, expecting a severe brow beating about missing school. Hopefully he would be sent home ...

Mr O'Donovan was a strict but fair Principal. A well-dressed gentleman who loved wearing leisure suits with a white belt and matching white shoes; he had thick square-framed glasses that brushed the edge of his long sideburns. Speaking with a strong Irish accent Mr O'Donovan was a funny man with a round red face, like a rosy apple.

'*Sir?*' JJ asked as he entered the office.

'*Ah JJ, good morning. Now I am sorry to drop this on you as I was planning on speaking to you last week, but I hear you weren't so well.*' Mr O'Donovan cleared his throat and put his head down. JJ realized that he wasn't going to be reprimanded for skipping school after all and relaxed a little.

'Now then. Do you remember the 'buddy system' we had in place when you started?' he asked.

'Yes sir,' JJ answered.

'Grand! Well, here's the thing. We have a young lad starting here today, name's Jeremiah Freeman. He has a few problems. Well, what I mean is that the lad is in a wheelchair and struggles with his eyesight.'

'Why? What's wrong with him?' JJ asked, frowning. 'And what's this got to do with me?' he wondered.

'Maybe you can ask him yourself?'

'Is he blind?' JJ asked, hardly believing what he was hearing. To be in a wheelchair was one thing but blind too!

'No, not blind, just hasn't got perfect vision. He's a funny guy. Think you will like him. I want you to be his buddy, show him the ropes and all,' Mr O'Donovan explained.

JJ's heart sank. The last thing he needed was any more attention being drawn to him, which this boy inevitably would do. Why did they pick on him to do it? What was wrong with any of the others? What rotten luck! The story of his life!

'You don't look so sure now, JJ?' Mr O'Donovan said, a

little concerned.

'I just don't see why I gotta do it, sir. How come the others can't,' he reasoned.

'You're the man for the job, JJ, I know it.'

JJ wasn't stupid. He was convinced he'd been chosen because he didn't have any friends.

'Well, I guess I have to then, don't I?' he said with a heavy heart.

Mr O'Donovan jumped up enthusiastically and went to the door. JJ was definitely NOT expecting what happened next when a few minutes later Jeremiah Freeman wheeled himself into the office. He was African–American, with tight curly black hair and a huge beaming smile on his face. His wheelchair was brightly colored and had American flags painted all over it.

'What's he got to look so happy about?' JJ thought but fortunately didn't ask.

'Jeremiah Freeman – or Jerry, I believe you like to be called? I'd like you to meet Josiah Mahoney, who likes to be known as JJ.' Mr O'Donovan introduced the two boys.

Jerry beamed at JJ and put his hand out to shake.

JJ reluctantly shook the boy's hand.

'This is almost the worst day of my life,' he thought.

'Do either of you have any questions you have for each other?' Mr O'Donovan asked.

'No, sir,' JJ said.

'I got millions, sir, but I'll save 'em for later. So JJ, you wanna show me where our class is? Maybe if Mr O'Donovan can wheel the chair, you can give me a piggy-back ride?'

JJ looked horrified and Jerry burst out laughing and started maneuvering himself with perfect ease and grace. Obviously sensing JJ's reluctance, Jerry thought to make a joke of it.

'It's cool, JJ, I was just kidding. I can still use my arms, see.' With that, Jerry threw his arms high in the air and swung them round and around.

The day panned out unexpectedly. JJ found him-self in the unfamiliar territory of being left alone by the bullies. The other children were suspicious of Jerry. Damon and Jenny had laughed at him when he and JJ first got to class but Mrs Horlick and Mr O'Donovan had obviously given them all a pep talk, so they were mainly polite.

Lunchtime was difficult. JJ had to make space for Jerry's chair and since Jerry couldn't reach the counter, JJ had to get his lunch too. By the time he returned to the table with his own lunch his heart sank. Damon and Jenny were sitting next to Jerry.

'So, is it true you can die any minute?' Damon asked.

'Yeah, is it true?' Jenny echoed.

JJ felt so sorry for Jerry but didn't have it in him to stand up for him. Turns out, JJ had nothing to worry about. Jeremiah Freeman was more than able to stick up for himself. Jerry decided to deal with them both, using his unique sense of humor. He took a mouthful of food and pretended to choke, he then pretended to pass out and crossed his eyes and dribbled out of the side of his mouth. JJ was momentarily stunned as Damon and Jenny started squealing for help. Jerry opened his eyes and winked at JJ and the two boys burst out laughing.

Damon was furious at having the tables turned on him but instead of doing what he would normally do and take it out on JJ, out of character, he walked away embarrassed, with Jenny in his wake.

JJ and Jerry dug into their food. They ate in silence for a while before JJ couldn't bear the silence any longer.

'That never happened before, you know,' JJ said.

'What?' Jerry asked.

'Somebody not scared of Damon,' JJ explained.

'Well, let's face it, JJ, what's the worst he can do, I mean a big tough guy like him can hardly pick on a cripple, can he? Hey, don't flinch. I'm allowed to call myself that, besides it helps me deal with it. Now come on! Let's get outside.' Jerry spun his wheelchair around and started to leave the cafeteria and JJ ran to keep up.

'Hey, JJ, let's do some wheelies,' Jerry suggested.

'Wheelies?'

'Sure. Push as fast as you can and then grip holda the handles and take your feet off and put them on those foot rests you see on the bottom. Come on, go!' Jerry shouted.

JJ did as he was told and the two boys had the time of their lives. As the wheelchair picked up speed JJ thought of his forthcoming trip to the theme park. How exhilarating it was going to be to ride the Big Bend. He jumped on the back of the chair just as Mr O'Donovan appeared around the corner.

'Josiah Mahoney, those foot rests are for tilting the chair to lift over things, NOT for standing on,' he said. He tried to sound stern but secretly he was delighted to see the bond forming between these two boys already. Still, he was concerned for Jerry's safety and asked for reassurance that Jerry would not fall out of his chair in his risky fearless reckless stunts.

Jerry told him that he and his Pa did wheelies all the time, which seemed to make Mr O'Donovan relax again.

'OK now, well be sure to be careful,' he told them.

The boys both nodded but couldn't quite hide their giggles.

They got to the main doors and JJ looked out.

'Oh man, I hate this hot weather,' he complained.

'Just now you were complaining about cold winters, make up your mind! Come on, let's get outta here,' Jerry said, as he turned to wheel his chair and open the large glass doors. JJ could see he was struggling and pushed forward to open them.

The Texas sun was scorching today. JJ really hated the sunshine but realized that Jerry had been right.

He had just been complaining about winter.

'Mind if we sit on the porch under the awning? he suggested, hoping Jerry would agree to a little shade.

'Yeah, if you can get this thing up there,' Jerry said.

'There's a ramp.'.

'Cool, we can use it as our launch pad into space,' Jerry said.

'Or we can pretend we're on a roller coaster?'

'Sure, let's do that.'

'Jerry?'

'Yeah?'

'Um, well how come... how come you...' JJ couldn't finish.

'OK, JJ, let's get this done with. 'Cuz I don't see too good, I walked in front of a truck and been in one of these ever since. Now don't go all soft on me, come on, let's go.' With that Jeremiah Freeman spun around and called for JJ to catch him up.

The two boys spent the rest of their lunch break doing just that, whizzing down the ramp and spinning the chair onto the concrete playground and finishing with a huge wheelie. All the other kids watched in wonder at the new partnership. JJ knew that it was only a matter of time before Damon snapped out of it and started bullying him again, but he was enjoying the respite all the same.

Over the next few weeks, JJ and Jerry became real buddies. They managed to fill each break with thrilling never-tried-before moves that took JJ's breath away. For the first time in his life he actually looked forward to school.

The first Friday in May was a special day for JJ. Besides being invited to Jerry's house for the evening, he had the added bonus of spending the rest of the weekend with his grandparents. Grandpa Joe had agreed to pick JJ up at 7pm. He had also arranged with Bernadette and his Pa for JJ to stay Saturday again.

JJ was so nervous as he approached Jerry's

front door because he had never been invited over to another kid's house before. But he had nothing to fear. Jerry's Ma opened the door and beamed at him. Pulling JJ into her arms she gave him the biggest hug that almost crushed him. This was definitely going to be an adventure.

'Now let me take a good look at you.' And she roughly pushed him back to arm's length. *'Yep, just as he described.'*

'Ma, put JJ down, you'll go and scare him off, then how am I gonna get around?' Jerry shouted from behind. Mrs Freeman told the boys to go and play while she got a snack ready for them. JJ followed Jerry into the most amazing bedroom he had ever seen. There was even a TV!

They had given Jerry an enormous room downstairs with its own bathroom and patio. It had been carefully designed with ramps and bars to help Jerry get around as independently as possible.

Every square inch of wall space was covered with posters of all JJ's favorite superheroes. It appeared that Jerry loved them too.

For a few minutes, JJ found it hard to hide his envy.

His home was nothing like the Freemans' and Jerry's bedroom was way more cool than his own. But when he saw Jerry struggle to lift himself out of his chair and onto his bench, he felt ashamed of himself. Here was a boy who had trouble seeing properly, who would probably never walk again, and yet never complained about the hand that life had dealt him.

'JJ, did you bring your baseball cards? I got a few we can trade, if you want?' Jerry asked as he started placing his cards on the table. JJ grabbed his from his pocket and went and sat beside Jerry to look. It was sometime later that Jerry's Ma called them through for their snack.

JJ was shocked by the size of Jerry's Pa. He was tall and broad, like Jackson. He had the blackest skin that JJ had ever seen, way blacker than Jerry's or his Ma's – and just like them he had the kind of smile that lit up a room.

'So, JJ, Jerry tells us you pull a mean wheelie, huh? Better than me apparently. Maybe we will take it outside once we've eaten, what do you reckon, huh?' he asked.

'Yes, sir,' JJ said, blushing.

'Benjamin! Call me Benjamin, my boy, not sir; makes me feel all official.'

Enjoying the cool evening breeze the four of them snacked and chatted about their day. JJ had no need to have been nervous because the Freeman family was so friendly they couldn't have made him feel more welcome.

Benjamin and Rebecca Freeman were hilarious. JJ could see where Jerry got his sense of humor. They cracked jokes, told amazing stories and treated their son as though he were just like any other ten-year-old boy. JJ wondered if perhaps this had helped Jerry remain optimistic and upbeat, against so many odds.

By the time Grandpa Joe arrived, the four of them were sitting outside in the fading sun enjoying an ice-cold soda. Grandpa accepted one and sat relaxing and chatting.

JJ was reminded again of yet another reason why he loved his Grandpa. He just turned up and mixed with people. It never mattered to Grandpa Joe what color their skin was, what country they were from or that Jerry was in a wheelchair. He just treated everyone the same.

They got home and Grandma May already had dinner ready. The three of them sat and chatted all about JJ's time with Jerry. Grandpa and Grandma were delighted by the event.

By the time JJ got to bed, his mind was racing. He was missing Toby like crazy, but his Pa had promised to drop him off tomorrow before going to the store.

JJ lay in bed thinking about Jerry. He couldn't get over his positive attitude. He would rather talk about his 'ability' than his 'disability'. Refusing to allow his physical condition to hold him back, Jerry seemed to love life and the world around him. He even liked school! Earlier that evening Jerry had played the keyboard and trumpet, in a way that sent shivers down JJ's spine.

When JJ had asked him how he got so good at playing, Jerry had smiled and said: *'A while back I spent a long time in the hospital. It gets kinda boring, so I taught myself how to play the trumpet and then Pa showed me how to play the keyboard.'*

JJ was in awe of his exceptional new friend. He cringed now as he remembered his response when Mr O'Donovan had asked him to buddy up with Jerry on Monday. JJ hoped Jerry didn't notice.

CHAPTER 7:

DREAM VACATION

Annual vacations were to the Mahoney family a special not-to-be-missed event. Although only lasting seven days, the whole family were involved in the planning for months. Once Christmas was over the family vacation became a hot topic of conversation. In the car, around the meal table, it was all JJ could find to talk about.

Normally Bernadette, Pa and Hannah would use an old World War II army surplus tent and JJ and Hannah would take it in turns to sleep in the Airstream camper with their grandparents. But this year they got to borrow the camper all for themselves as Grandpa Joe and Grandma May would sadly not be joining them. These Airstreams are THE WORLD'S COOLEST CARAVANS. Bullet-like sleek and shiny they glittered in the Texas sun. Originally built in LA they were an icon of the open road.

Vacations were always a family event; Grandpa and Grandma, Pa and Bernadette, JJ and Hannah along with Toby, much to Bernadette's disapproval. Although JJ had noted that she was becoming quite fond of the little mutt, even allowing him to stay indoors.

The family always travelled in two vehicles: Grandpa's

immaculate 1947 green Chevrolet pickup, that JJ loved to ride in, and Pa's 1960s Ford station wagon. Dark blue with pretend wooden side panels. Three rows of red and cream vinyl seats and drop down tailgate, giving access to enough room for all the family's needs. Although this old beater did little to improve JJ's street cred.

JJ couldn't wait to get to school to see Jerry and was disappointed to find he was out sick. JJ felt a sense of fear also, as he realized that without his new friend, the attention would be back on him.

Damon, realizing the same came straight up to JJ.

'Hey, Shorty, what did ya do to him, tip him outta his chair?' Damon asked, spitefully.

'You're not funny, Damon,' JJ responded bravely.

'So come on then, where is he? Dead?' Damon was finding himself highly amusing by now.

Poor JJ wanted to stand up to Damon for Jerry's sake, but knew what would happen if he did, so he tried walking away. Fortunately Mrs Horlick came into the class and Damon backed down.

JJ bumped into Mr O'Donovan in the corridor and

asked if he knew where Jerry was.

'Yes, his Mom called by, said he's not so well today, having a day in bed, should be back tomorrow.'

'Thank you, sir,' JJ said respectfully and walked slowly back to class.

When Jerry didn't appear the next day or the next, JJ started getting worried and asked Bernadette if she would take him over to see him.

Bernadette and JJ chatted comfortably on the drive to Jerry's. Bernadette felt so happy that JJ had asked her instead of his Pa to take him to see his friend. She knew it was too early to know for sure; however things really were becoming quite different at home and already she had seen a remarkable difference in JJ and knew Jerry was a big part of that change.

Jerry's Ma beamed at JJ and pulled him in for a huge hug.

'Why, it's my boy's best buddy. You come in and find my boy's smile 'cuz it's been upside down all week, he's been a real grump!' Turning to Bernadette, she said, *'You must be JJ's Ma, come in, I just made some coffee.'*

Bernadette shook hands with Mrs Freeman.

She instantly liked this kind-hearted woman with her enormous smile. She had seen her in church; however, she hadn't had a chance to introduce herself yet.

'You know the way, JJ. I'll bring you both some soda and cookies in a little while.'

JJ knocked gently on Jerry's bedroom door.

'Come in,' Jerry shouted. As soon as he realized it was JJ, his whole face lit up like a Christmas tree.

'JJ, I missed you, man, here, come sit down.'

JJ noticed that Jerry flinched in pain as he tried to move himself over to make room for his friend. JJ had brought along a bag of candy and a comic. Jerry was delighted and grateful. The two boys sat for a while in silence. Jerry, JJ realized, enjoyed silences, whereas they usually made JJ feel awkward.

'So what's wrong with you?' JJ asked his friend.

'Got some weird thing wrong with my back. Doc Mason said I gotta rest it but man, I was SO bored I even chopped beans for Ma. That's the worst thing about all this, I kinda get laid up sometimes and there's so much I wanna do,' Jerry explained, as though he merely had a slight cold, not a condition that would keep him in a wheelchair for

the rest of his life.

'I brought my baseball cards,' JJ said, reaching for them.

'Cool, let's see if we have any more we can trade. Do ya mind gettin' mine for me? Ma will blow a gasket it I get up. They're next to my baseball bat,' Jerry said nodding to where they were.

JJ got up and caught his breath. He had only known the boy for a few weeks but already he relied on their friendship and was shocked by how ill Jerry looked. In spite of still managing a smile, his eyes had lost all their sparkle.

Damon had said that his Pa told him that people like Jerry didn't live long and JJ was terrified that he was about to lose his friend.

Jerry seemed to have developed a sixth sense, and knew there was something wrong with JJ. He had known all about JJ being bullied and not wanting to buddy him. Mr O'Donovan had sworn Jerry's Ma to keep it quiet, but Rebecca had wanted to share it with her son in the hope that Jerry could help JJ as much as JJ was trying to help him. She had also told Jerry that JJ's Ma had died giving birth to JJ. Jerry could imagine the sadness deep inside JJ and wanted to help.

'*What's up with you today, JJ?*' he asked.

'*Nothin,*' JJ said.

'*Sure there is, you just don't wanna say it,*' Jerry said, revealing the same skills Grandpa Joe had of knowing when things weren't quite right.

'*Damon been at you?*' Jerry asked.

'*Yeah, but it's not that,*' JJ said, and then decided he wanted to change the subject, but Jerry was having none of it.

'*Look, you need to tell me 'cuz I know what it does*

to you when you store stuff up.' Jeremiah Freeman was years wiser than his age.

'I, I, well I was kinda worried about you 'cuz Damon said people like you don't live long.' JJ managed to spit the words out and Jerry astonished him by bursting out laughing.

'Ah, that boy's got one heck of an imagination. I'm good, JJ. Some kids got it lots worse than me. I'm lucky. Now, stop your worrying and stop listenin' to Damon, he sure is stupid 'n the sooner you see that, the better. He's a coward, JJ, all bullies are cowards, you just gotta learn to ignore them.' Jerry smiled and heaved himself up straighter, signalling that the conversation was now over.

'Lucky, LUCKY!' JJ thought. Only Jeremiah Freeman would see himself as lucky.

When it was time to go, JJ felt happier, not only because the two boys hadn't stopped laughing, but mainly because Jerry looked so much brighter. Even Mrs Freeman said how much better he looked and invited him to drop by the next day.

School the following day was bearable because Damon was off sick and JJ had the added bonus of looking forward to dropping by Jerry's later. Tomorrow was Friday and JJ would be staying at

Grandpa Joe's and visiting Jackson's ranch. Then on Saturday he would see Scarlett O'Hara, his new equine buddy. Perfect!

JJ smiled to himself now, amazed that in just a few weeks his life had improved so much. He didn't feel right talking about Scarlett O'Hara and his upcoming family vacation with Jerry. He realized that some days, like today, Jerry's whole world was within four walls. And even when he did get out it wasn't long before he would need to go home due to being exhausted or needing more medication.

Jerry knew his friend was keeping stuff from him. Sometimes people felt guilty when they could do stuff that was physically beyond him. He wanted JJ to know that real friends can talk about everything. But JJ was a tough nut to crack.

Jerry's Ma insisted on asking questions over supper that night. She asked JJ what his plans were for the weekend and he put his head down, nervously.

'I stay with my Grandpa Joe and Grandma May on Fridays, then I go help at a ranch on Saturdays and get to... um brush a horse there and... um maybe I will get to ride her someday.' There, he had said it. He blushed scarlet.

'Oh man, I'd love to ride a horse, please Ma,' Jerry asked.

'Jeremiah Freeman, have you completely lost your senses, you silly boy, of course you can't ride no horse.' She and Jerry's Pa were laughing.

'So can I go watch JJ when he starts to ride then?' he asked.

'Of course you can. Well, if it's OK. You wouldn't mind, JJ, would you?' Jerry's Pa asked.

'No, sir, I... I just feel bad.' 'Oops, that slipped out,' JJ thought.

'Bad about what?' Mr Freeman asked.

'Nothin', sir,' JJ said.

'Well bless you, JJ. Now don't go keepin' stuff in, makes it come out real messy. What's up?' Rebecca said gently.

'I don't like it that Jerry can't do stuff, Ma'am, makes me feel bad,' JJ said so bravely.

Jerry, his Ma and Pa all started laughing and Rebecca jumped up to hug him.

'Don't you go worryin' about my boy. Trust me, what he lacks in his physical abilities, he sure makes up elsewhere. Jerry goes places in his mind that the rest of us can only *dream of, ain't that right, honey?'* she said. Jerry was laughing but reached over and patted JJ gently on the back.

'Trust me, man, I'm good, now enough with the pity and please pass me some more pie.'

The rest of the evening went great. Jerry, JJ and Mr and Mrs Freeman played baseball in the yard. They improvised well and Jerry was exceptional at batting. JJ noticed how careful Mr Freeman was at pitching to Jerry, who had been forced to wear every type of protective clothing known to humankind.

JJ was pleasantly surprised when his Pa, Bernadette and Hannah came to pick him up. They were persuaded to join in making the team bigger. Jerry eventually retired to the porch with a blanket and his milk and cookies, but was loudly cheering them all on. He was so much better today.

Before the Mahoneys left, Jerry's Ma asked them to come over for dinner after church on Sunday. JJ was thrilled that they accepted. Bernadette and Mrs Freeman got along great and JJ knew that Bernadette and his Pa were making an enormous effort for him.

That night in his journal JJ wrote:

THURSDAY

Had the best night, me, Pa, Bernadette, Piglet and Jerry and his folks all played bassball. Jerry can really hit! we got asked to dinner Sunday and Bernadette's gonna make some of her lemonade to take. Don't hate Bernadette anymore don't hate Piglet either. I can't wait 'til tomorrow to tell Grandpa Joe all about today. I'm going to bed now. I hope Damon is still out sick tomorrow.

Sleep didn't come easy that evening. JJ's mind was working over. He just couldn't contain his excitement at the thought that school would be out in just one more week. The count-down had begun. Just six more days of school before they went on the vacation of a lifetime. Nine more sleeps and they'd be off. When sleep refused to take him to his peaceful place, he pictured Grandpa Joe, sitting on the porch and reading to him. Within minutes he had drifted off to sleep with a huge smile on his face.

CHAPTER 8:

THE BIG BEND

JJ had the best week at school. Not only was Damon off for the entire week but Jerry was back too. The two boys played theme parks all week. The ramp leading up to the porch outside the art room became the perfect roller coaster climb. The boys' imaginations provided them with the lights and music. In fact by the end of the week the entire playground had become a magical theme park. The rest of the school watched, bewildered as JJ and Jerry rushed from ride to ride in their invisible theme park.

Back home, JJ had used planks of wood, barrels, anything he could get his hands on to create his very own roller coaster. He would sit on his bike and pretend he was getting strapped into his seat on Big Bend and then, with the sprinkling of a little fairy dust, he was off. His imagination did not disappoint him. Poor Toby was jealous because he wasn't getting JJ's undivided attention for once. He watched the boy with a confused expression on his face and no wag in his tail at all.

Bernadette watched from the window, smiling at the change in JJ. She was proud of the way the family had united in helping JJ although she knew there was a way to go. Still, the difference in him was remarkable. She just hoped that JJ would be tall enough to pass the height restrictions and ride on the one roller coaster he was obsessed with. If not, she knew it would break his heart. She had told his Pa to gently warn JJ that there was a slight chance of not being tall enough, and that it was all for JJ's safety. However, it fell on deaf ears.

Visiting theme parks was certainly not Hannah's idea of fun, but she knew how much it meant to JJ, so she went along with it. Besides, last year she had chosen where she wanted to go so it seemed only fair. Hannah had a soft spot for her half brother even though he insisted on calling her Piglet. Most of the time she felt sorry for JJ, but sometimes he was just plain annoying.

She even wondered what it would be like to have a brother who had to live life in a wheelchair! Sometimes life seemed complicated.

Bernadette dried her hands and then took JJ out a glass of lemonade and a cookie. Toby bounced up to her and she patted his head and smiled. She was actually becoming quite fond of the little dog if she was honest with herself.

'JJ, here's a snack, buddy. I need to go pack for your Pa and I. I put all your clothes and suitcase on your bed and all you gotta do is pack it and choose your books and toys. Let me know if you need me, and don't get too hot.'

'Thanks, Bernadette,' JJ said as he drained the glass of lemonade and stuffed the cookie into his mouth. Toby scrambled around, desperate to snatch up even the smallest crumb.

Jerry's folks brought him over that evening to say good-bye and Bernadette insisted on them staying for coffee. They didn't have a ramp for Jerry and the porch steps were pretty high so they moved the table and chairs down onto the driveway so everyone could sit together. Toby jumped up onto Jerry's lap and started licking all round the boy's ears making Jerry squeal with delight.

'Oh, I'm so sorry! JJ! Get him down! He could hurt Jerry,' Bernadette shouted; she was so worried that Jerry would get injured but his folks seemed to find it funny.

'Please don't stress, Bernadette, Jerry's got three blankets over his lap and Toby's so small, he should be fine,' Mrs Freeman said.

'Are you sure, Jerry?' Bernadette asked, still worried.

'Sure, please don't move him, he's cool,' Jerry said. Eventually Toby settled down and curled up and fell fast asleep on Jerry's lap.

JJ was overwhelmed with happiness. He felt so normal having a friend and his folks come visit and it was clear that his folks and Jerry's were becoming good friends. Even Jerry and Hannah got along really well, which surprised JJ since he really didn't get girls at all.

When it was time to go, the two boys high-fived one another. The Mahoneys stood and waved as the Freemans drove off. As the dust cloud created by the Freemans' vehicle began to settle, JJ realized that he was going to miss his best buddy. However, happy thoughts of their trip were almost overwhelming and so he decided he needed to pack and get to bed so morning would come sooner.

The excitement of packing and preparing for this vacation did, however, hold a tinge of sadness. For the first time ever Grandpa, Grandma and Toby would not be joining them. Way behind on a pressing deadline, Grandpa had no option but to stay at home working on his latest manuscript. Grandma May had been secretly relieved, since the thought of long lines at theme parks, in this heat, was not her idea of a vacation at all. However, she didn't want to disappoint JJ, so she hid her feelings.

JJ didn't drift off to sleep until the early hours. It didn't even help to picture Grandpa reading to him. The time still dragged on forever. Even Toby got fed up with JJ's fidgeting and moved onto the floor to sleep.

JJ wondered if Hannah was struggling to sleep too. He couldn't go check on her since the creaking floorboard outside her room could wake his folks. He knew Pa had a long drive ahead of him tomorrow and Bernadette had been working so hard to get everyone ready for their dream vacation.

In spite of only a couple of hours sleep, JJ woke surprisingly alert. He put his book on top of his clothes and a few other things in the suitcase. He had packed so much stuff in his bag that he needed to sit on it in order to buckle it up before carrying it down stairs.

Pa had already picked up Grandpa's camper, which was now hitched to their car. So he was now trying to pack it neatly. Bernadette was frying some bacon. She smiled at JJ and gave him some cold milk.

'Here, JJ, it will settle your stomach for the trip. We are all gonna have some bacon and eggs, would you like to try some?' she asked, concerned since JJ often got car sick.

JJ decided he was starving and that it was worth the risk. The four of them sat down together chatting. Everyone was in good spirits. Toby, sensing something was different, kept shaking and making an annoying whining noise.

'Silly mutt, you'll love it when you see who you get a whole week with. He'll be spoiled rotten by the time we get back,' Pa said to them all. Toby calmed down a little as though he had actually understood every word.

At that moment they could hear Grandpa's truck coming up the drive to pick up Toby. Grandpa gave Hannah a huge hug before turning to JJ.

'Remember, buddy, you make notes and get your Pa to take pictures so I can see it all,' he said.

'I love you, Grandpa, I'm gonna miss you,' JJ said with tears in his eyes.

'I'm hopin' you'll be too busy to miss anybody, now go, git! Remember to write it down. I want smells, sounds, lights, music. I want you to capture it all so's Grandma May and I don't feel left out, ya hear!'

JJ hugged Grandma May who insisted on loudly planting kisses all over his cheeks, smothering him in lipstick and finding herself most amusing.

They headed first to Astro World in Houston. Pa had reserved a spot at a recreational vehicle park nearby, but to JJ and Hannah each mile seemed to take forever. Hannah was good company and she had made up some pretty cool games to play on the journey, but they just couldn't get there quick enough.

Pa had to stop twice for gas, a restroom break and to get everyone something to drink. One of the truck stops had the coolest diner created from an old railway carriage that made you feel as if you were taking a train ride to your destination. So the four of them had an early lunch before setting off again. They found the campground and spent the next three days visiting the theme park and riding on everything. Hannah wasn't usually a fan of theme parks and neither was Bernadette. But it was worth it to see JJ clearly having the time of his life. There was plenty for them to enjoy as well. Pa and JJ even found time to play catch and the whole family would enjoy a game of frisbee.

It was proving to be a special vacation for everyone. In the evenings, Pa would help Bernadette cook around the campfire while JJ and Hannah explored nearby. Later after supper, they all played ball or hide and seek.

After Astro World they made their way to Six Flags Over Texas and the legendary Big Bend roller coaster.

If JJ had found the first leg of the journey hard, this next one was proving impossible. Another 239 miles. Pa had made sure they set off at 5am to get set up at the next campground, so they could have the whole afternoon at Six Flags. But it seemed like the whole world was heading to Arlington. It took forever.

Each minute seemed to drag for JJ as he kept picturing Big Bend and wondering if he would even get to see it today, let alone ride it. He closed his eyes and prayed silently that he would.

JJ's excitement kept colliding with his insecurities and it was exhausting. He was so frightened, too – not that he was frightened of the stomach churning experience that all adrenaline junkies longed for. His fear was based on the fact that he just might not measure up. All roller coasters had a height restriction for the safety of the passengers. Too small and you can't ride!

They arrived at their next RV park, which was in JJ's mind even greater than the last. They found their reserved space, with electric hook up, under the trees to shade them from the relentless sun. There was also a fresh running stream for the children to cool off in. JJ reflected that Toby would love it here; however he knew the little dog would be having the time of his life with Grandpa Joe and Grandma May. Toby was the only other being that was allowed to enter World HQ when Grandpa was working and usually spent his time either curled up on Grandpa's lap, or at his feet.

They all unpacked as quickly as they could but JJ was impatient to leave, so Bernadette made snacks, allowing them to waste no more time and to eat on the way.

Arriving at the park, JJ couldn't keep still. He and Pa got in line; neither Bernadette nor Hannah were interested in joining them. They decided to ride something tamer than this enormous intimidating monster ride.

The only concern JJ had now, as he stood in line was would he measure up? Right before you got to the ride, he could see his tormentor teasing him, threatening him just like Damon. This time, however, his tormentor was a measuring rod that you had to stand against to prove that you were tall enough. He watched as other kids were told to stand against it and for each one just big enough to ride, there were as many being turned away. JJ told himself that they were way younger and smaller than him, but he was scared all the same.

JJ had succeeded in reaching the required height at the previous theme park and from a distance he was pretty sure that this one didn't look any higher, but he was so apprehensive that he would come up short. He could hardly stand the suspense! The nearer he got to the ride the more his confidence began to falter. Waiting in a line that kept folding back on itself was sheer agony. It reminded him of school, waiting to be picked for the team and yet knowing it was unlikely.

Eventually they made it to the end of the line and there it was. He so wished he had some platform shoes to wear rather than these sneakers.

Then his moment arrived. Pa squeezed his shoulder as the park attendant gestured for JJ to come over to be measured.

'Go on, buddy, you'll be fine,' Pa said. As he cautiously walked over he stared directly at his tormentor. As he got

closer it seemed to grow further out of his reach.

He stood tall against the measuring stick. Stretching himself as upright as a short ten year old could, he waited for the verdict.

'Sorry, bud, maybe next time,' the park attendant casually told him. 'Next time, there's no next time, it has to be now', JJ thought to himself.

Once again, JJ had come up short. Devastation and despair overwhelmed JJ and there was nothing he could do about it.

Pa asked the attendant to call the park officials, where he tried for several moments to persuade them that JJ was almost tall enough, but they refused to let him on Big Bend.

'They let him ride the roller coaster at Astro World and it's really about the same as this one, and he was tall enough there!' Pa couldn't have tried harder to persuade the park officials to change their minds. But it was no good. JJ just didn't measure up!

Crushed, with his head bowed and shoulders slumped low, JJ shuffled away from the line. Dreams shattered, hopes dead, his ego once again broken. 'Why, oh why, did I blab to my classmates about beating Big

Bend? The sneering voices rang in his head ... *'Hey, don't forget to take your Mama's heels, or they won't let you on, Shorty.'*

Once again he was full of that feeling of someone who didn't meet the approval of others. Because he was so short, he was unacceptable to the standard set by those around him. JJ felt that he was and always would be a loser.

JJ was inconsolable. Nothing his Pa said or did seemed to help. He so wished at this moment that Grandpa were here. He would understand. He would know what to say. He would help him to think straight.

Never had JJ needed his Grandpa more. He squeezed his eyes tight, desperate to calm himself down before he had one of his temper tantrums in front of all these people. He kept repeating Grandpa's promise. *'Close your eyes and picture me and I will be right there beside you.'* And there he was, typing away on Old Faithful with Toby curled up on his lap and Grandma May bringing a plate of sandwiches since he would be too busy to break for food.

JJ smiled just for a moment as he felt the warmth of Grandpa's love. It was just what he needed. Grandpa Joe was his constant safe place in his tough world.

But how could he face everyone after this enormous failure to achieve his goal? He didn't get to ride on Big Bend. He didn't measure up after all.

CHAPTER 9:

GRANDPA'S GATE

Distraught, JJ dejectedly shuffled from the scene of his most shameful experience yet. This was the worst moment of his life. His world had ended.

Eventually Pa and JJ managed to find Bernadette and Hannah. Hannah couldn't bear to see her brother so upset. She offered him her cotton candy but JJ rudely shoved it away. When Bernadette reached out her arms to hug him he stepped sideways and made a beeline for the exit.

'JJ, wait,' his Pa shouted.

'Leave him be, hun, he's been plannin' on riding that

monster since Christmas, he's gonna be devastated,'
Bernadette said sadly.

*'Well, it's no excuse for him to be rude and spoil everybody
else's vacation, is it?'* Pa said.

JJ didn't say a word. He spent the entire journey back
to the RV park picturing Grandpa Joe and wishing he
was at home. He knew how busy Grandpa was and that
right now the gate leading to World HQ would be firmly
shut.

Surrounded with a dry stone wall there was only one
way that led to the winding path up to where Grandpa
worked. When busy, the gate would be closed and no
one, absolutely no one was allowed to disturb Josiah
James Mahoney I. The writing genius would be deep
in thought and visitors were an unwelcome distraction.
That is, except his grandchildren!

World HQ was set in the middle of a grassy meadow
at the rear of Grandpa Joe's colonial-styled house.
Gathered from around the property, boulder-sized
stones had been piled up to form the wall. Although
there was no warning sign it made a clear statement:
'No Trespassers'. The only form of access was a break
in the wall, in which a wooden gate had been placed.

Although never locked it was a further sign that unwelcome visitors should keep out.

The old wooden gate, with crackled paint baked and blistered by the hot Texan sun, would never separate JJ from his Grandpa. JJ had learnt a long time ago to ignore the wall and gate, knowing Grandpa would stop everything when his grandchildren called. Positioned just above JJ's maximum height the sign read: 'No one taller that this may enter'. Here was someone with whom he would never 'come up short'. Here was a place he could find acceptance, appreciation and acknowledgment as a much-loved child. Grandpa's loving embrace would sweep him off the ground and make him feel good about himself deep to the very core of his inner being.

Biting back the tears, JJ hardly waited for the station wagon to stop before jumping out and escaping down to the stream.

'Do you think I should go after him? I know it's safe 'cuz I checked it out earlier but...?' Pa asked Bernadette.

'Do you know what, hun, I really think we should let him be. He's managed to get himself back here without an outburst. That's something of a miracle. Maybe let sleeping dogs lie. His dream has turned into a horrible nightmare. We can see him from here. Let's get set up and when ready we can call him for dinner,' Bernadette said kindly to her husband.

Bernadette and Pa began to unload the Airstream. Having put up the awning, they set about lighting a campfire. Hannah retired with her book. She felt so sorry for JJ and desperately wanted to comfort him. But she knew he wouldn't appreciate it. She knew that

JJ always took everything so personally. She prayed that one day her brother would find the kind of love and acceptance taught in Sunday School of a Heavenly Father who loved us no matter what.

Hannah thought of Damon and the others. She hoped they would never find out that JJ wasn't big enough to ride on Big Bend. They would bully and ridicule him for months. Bullying may have made them feel big, but it made JJ feel small. They might find it amusing but Hannah didn't think it was funny at all.

She looked across to the stream. She could just about see him. '*I wish Grandpa Joe were here,*' she sighed.

JJ sat gazing into the stream. He could hear some bigger boys shouting further down the stream. They had made a swing out of an old tire and took turns riding it. He watched enviously as they swung way up high into the sky before plummeting down and then flying back up the other side. It was just the sort of adrenalin-fuelled ride that JJ loved.

JJ decided to move a little closer so that he could get a better look but was cautious, because he didn't want to attract too much attention to himself. He must have sat for an hour watching the boys swinging back and forth.

Eventually the fun ceased. One of the boys took such a long run up from the high banks above the stream that he almost did a complete loop. Unfortunately this did not bode well for the swing as it got hooked on the end of the branch.

The boy fell but fortunately landed on the bank and not way down in the stream, which could have been messy. JJ watched as the boys tried desperately to unhook the rope from the end of the branch with long sticks. Two climbed up the tree and tried sliding along the branch to unhook it. They were big boys, easily sixteen years old, and the end of the branch was much thinner than the thick end they had attached the rope too. It creaked in protest warning them not to risk it, since it could not take their weight.

JJ felt a shadow above him. He looked up into the eyes of an enormous angry-looking boy. 'Oh no, here goes,' he thought, feeling himself grow hot.

'*Hey dude, you scared of heights?*' he asked.

'*No,*' JJ said, standing up. The older boy dwarfed him.

'*Would ya climb up there and untangle our swing? We'd owe you one,*' he asked.

JJ gulped. He knew Bernadette would worry about how high it was. He reasoned that even if he fell, he would maybe at worst break a bone or two. Suddenly he was filled with determination to accomplish just one thing in his life!

'Sure,' he said and followed the boy over to the others who were either the same size or even bigger.

If Grandpa Joe could see him now JJ knew he would be smiling and cheering him on. This thought filled him with courage as he looked up into the towering tree. He was up for the challenge.

The big boy who he now knew as Chuck, introduced JJ to the other enormous guys. They all looked angry and unimpressed that Chuck had asked this 'squirt' of a guy to help. JJ spat into his palms and rubbed his hands together. This wasn't the time to retreat. He really couldn't take any more disappointment today. He had to do this! He just had to!

He climbed up the tree behind Chuck. As they reached the branch holding the rope swing JJ started to step out onto it but Chuck grabbed his arm.

'Wait! Dude, you can't just go out there.'

'*Why not? You did,*' JJ said bravely.

'*Sure, but man I'm way older than you. Here, let me tie this around your waist and I can chuck it over that branch a bit higher. You guys get ready to hold it, OK?*' he called out to the other boys. But with a sudden rush of clarity JJ knew that this wouldn't work.

'*I can do it without the rope*', he said, with much more confidence than he actually felt. It was one of those 'do or die' moments that made him feel like one of his own comic book heroes.

'Here goes,' he thought. JJ crawled slowly to the end of the branch. The journey seemed to go on forever. He had already been subjected to one agonizing trip today, waiting in line for Big Bend. What if he messed this up too? He made the mistake of looking down, which made him lose his balance. Just for a second he got so dizzy that he thought he would fall. Tears stung his eyes and he froze, unable to move at all.

'*You're OK, man,*' Chuck shouted. Obviously he had seen JJ nearly fall and lose his nerve. JJ knew he had to do this. He knew it was important to him that he rescued the swing. All the cool big boys were watching and cheering him on.

'You're almost there, man, keep going,' they shouted from the high banks.

'Dude, you're safe,' another shouted. JJ found the novelty of having praise shouted rather than taunts a refreshing change and just for a moment, it was like he could hear Grandpa Joe talking to him: *'You can do this, JJ, you can do this, I'm with you.'*

All of a sudden he felt a surge of strength tingle through his entire body. He pushed forward. He channeled every ounce of fear, very much aware that the diminishing branch was beginning to move slightly. Chuck was constantly reassuring him that it would hold JJ's weight and he was right.

After what seemed a lifetime, he finally got to the end of the branch. With all his might he stretched himself way beyond comfortable and after several attempts managed to unhook the rope, sending the tire sailing down. The boys all cheered and clapped for him and JJ had never felt so big in his life. He so wished that Damon and the others were here to see this.

True to his word Chuck had waited for him, coaching him back every step of the way. By the time JJ climbed down, all the enormous boys gathered round to pat him on the back and high-five him.

JJ beamed to himself, his face actually ached from smiling. He started to walk away.

'Hey, where you going, dude?' Chuck said.

'I... I guess I should go,' JJ said.

'No way, man! Don't you wanna try it?' Chuck said.

'Really? You mean it?' JJ asked, realizing how uncool he sounded and blushed scarlet. Chuck smiled kindly at him.

'Man, if it wasn't for you we wouldn't have it back, sure you can use it. Come on.'

JJ had the time of his life. The boys could not have made him feel more welcome. It didn't slip JJ's attention that they were very careful with him and didn't swing him

anywhere near as high as each other, but it was still an amazing adrenaline rush.

The five boys had come on vacation by themselves. Their families lived near the RV park and occasionally checked in on them. JJ envied them their freedom. How he longed for the day that he would be able to take a trip with a few friends. His heart sank as he realized his only friend back home was Jerry and he doubted Jerry could go camping.

Hannah came to find him to call him for dinner and saw who he was with. She had a feeling that JJ wouldn't want the big boys to see him being called to supper by his little sister, so she went back to camp and told Pa to go.

Pa was a little uneasy when he saw the age and size of the boys JJ was with. He was pleasantly surprised by how polite they all were and how they genuinely seemed to care for JJ.

Chuck high-fived JJ as he left.

'Hey, JJ,' he shouted. JJ and Pa stopped and looked round.

'We'll be here tomorrow if you wanna come back. We're gonna bring some food with us to save breakin' the day up,' Chuck said.

'Sure, I'd like that, thanks,' JJ said and then smiling he walked back to camp with Pa.

'Pa, would it be OK if we didn't go anywhere tomorrow? Can I just hang out with Chuck 'n them?' he pleaded.

'Of course you can, I'll bet Bernadette can make you a good lunch to take too so's you don't miss out,' Pa said smiling.

'Thanks, Pa, and Pa?' JJ said.

'Yes?'

JJ stared shyly into his Pa's eyes but then just said, 'Nothin'.

JJ wished he had the right words to let his Pa know he was OK. The worst day of his life had somehow turned out to be one of the best!

Pa had never wanted to hug his son more, but he managed to stop himself since he knew they were still in eyeshot of the others. JJ might feel embarrassed if his new friends saw him getting a much-needed hug from his Pa.

The next three days were the happiest days of JJ's life. They didn't go back to the amusement park, JJ didn't want to. Instead he spent every day with Chuck and his friends; they even invited Hannah to join in.

Bernadette made them all dinner on their last night and invited Chuck and his friends to join them. It was a magical evening. They sat around the campfire telling stories. JJ felt a lump in his throat that these new friends would never get to meet Grandpa Joe and hear his stories. 'Grandpa would love a night like tonight,' JJ thought.

When it was time to go, JJ fought back the tears but alas, he couldn't stop them. Chuck signaled for the others to go. They all patted JJ on the back.

'Hey, JJ, listen man. I have an aunt and uncle who live in Fredericksburg; your Pa was tellin' me it's only a few miles drive from Willow. We always come visit them each year so how about we hang out? I got a brother too, Dwain, he's only a year older than you, I think you'd like him. Anyway, dude, I gave your Ma my address and she gave me yours so I can write and let you know when we're coming, OK?'

JJ couldn't speak, he just mumbled. The tears were falling thick and fast now. He could not believe the kindness he had received from these guys, particularly Chuck.

As he tried to sleep that night he couldn't stop

thinking of getting home to Grandpa Joe and Jerry. He had begged his Pa to make a really safe swing in the yard for Jerry. He knew his best buddy would never experience the pure adrenalin rush of the tire swing but at least he would get to experience riding a swing.

With interest in the Big Bend beginning to fade, JJ was for the first time ever starting to feel thankful.

LIFE was a bit like a roller coaster. Full of surprising highs and lows, with a lot of twists and turns along the way. One minute JJ had no friends, now he had Jerry, Jackson, Chuck and the others. Life was changing for the better. Josiah James may not have experienced the thrill of riding the Big Bend, but he was discovering that family and friends were enjoyable in a different kind of way.

JJ couldn't wait to tell Grandpa Joe about his trip. Grandpa Joe would understand the disappointment and shame that still hovered at the back of his mind. Grandpa Joe would love the story of the tire swing. He would love to hear about the death-defying crawl along the thinnest branch in the world. Grandpa Joe would be glad that JJ had found some new friends. Grandpa Joe would understand everything.

He slept that night, having the most bizarre dream: he, Grandpa Joe, Chuck, Jerry and Jackson were all riding the Big Bend together on an old tire, holding on for dear life, but laughing and screaming, with Toby on Grandpa's lap.

CHAPTER 10:

FLYER IN THE SHED!

As Pa pulled the station wagon to a halt, JJ dived out and ran straight into Grandpa Joe's arms. Just being held by his Grandpa was enough to demolish all those defensive walls built up over his failure to ride Big Bend.

'Woah, let me take a look at you.' Grandpa Joe gently released him and looked at his grandson. 'My, you've got bigger in just a week,' he said before pulling him back into his arms.

Toby was frantically trying to get JJ's attention, ecstatic to see his favorite human again. Bernadette and Pa knew what their son needed most right now was his Grandpa and tried to calm the little dog down. Toby seemed to have expanded several inches in width since last week. Toby, like the rest of them, adored Grandma May's cooking.

Grandma May embraced the rest of the family and when JJ finally broke away from Grandpa and picked Toby up for a cuddle, Hannah got to have her hug with Grandpa Joe too.

The family went into the house to enjoy some iced tea and Grandma May's homemade cupcakes. They told them all about their adventure and no one mentioned Big Bend. So when they got up to leave, Grandpa Joe suggested the children and Toby stay with them for supper to give Ma and Pa a chance to unpack. Grandpa knew JJ needed to talk so he said he would run the three of them home later.

Grandma May and Hannah decided to do some baking and Grandpa Joe suggested he and JJ take Toby down for a quick walk to the stream that ran around the property, to cool off.

Grandpa Joe listened as JJ told him all about the disastrous attempt at riding Big Bend. He allowed the boy to pour his heart out and would gently squeeze his shoulder to encourage him to continue when he got too upset. JJ had been holding his rejection inside ever since the event. The rest of the holiday and the fun he had with Chuck and the others had been a welcome distraction from his fears of returning to school and to the total humiliation he felt by the whole Big Bend episode.

He hadn't felt safe enough to let his true feelings out but now that he was back in Grandpa's arms, he could hardly control the pain.

Grandpa Joe knew that this all went far deeper than not being able to ride the roller coaster. He knew it related to JJ's entire life of feeling like he never, ever measured up. He knew he needed to help JJ get to the next stage in his journey, so he could hopefully choose to become a winner who sometimes loses, not a loser who sometimes wins.

'OK, that's enough for Toby. Why don't we grab another cupcake and some lemonade and take it out to World HQ?' Grandpa Joe said, putting his arm around JJ's shoulders.

JJ couldn't wait to get inside World HQ. He had pictured it the entire week he had been away and couldn't wait to hear how Grandpa Joe's new book was going.

He knew Grandpa hadn't been able to come on their vacation because he was on a deadline to get the book off to his publisher. Now, he wanted to know how far he had gotten. Since Grandpa had written so many books, the topic was fascinating to JJ.

Over the last few months Grandpa had shared with JJ the story of Wilbur and Orville Wright. Two uneducated bicycle mechanics who, like JJ, had had a dream that nothing could quench. The story of the Wright Brothers is the stuff of childhood dreams, pioneers who found a way to show how the FORCE of lift could overcome the LAW of gravity. These two courageous brothers managed to break away from the limited small thinking of others, that said humans would never fly. And although at first they only flew a few feet off the ground, eventually they did manage to soar.

In some strange way the story of the Wright Brothers had gotten to JJ. 'Maybe his own dreams could come true? Perhaps one day he could overcome his own doubts? Who knows, he might even be able to prove his peers wrong too!'

On his desk, Grandpa Joe had a model of the plane that the Wright Brothers flew, called Flyer. JJ had often watched Grandpa pick the little plane up in his hands to study it. Sometimes he would stop his typing, pick it up and close his eyes. He could sit like that for several minutes before smiling, returning it to the desk and then getting straight back to work on his old typewriter. JJ believed that the plane had a way of connecting Grandpa Joe with those historic events that happened so long ago, because one minute he could be huffing and puffing and rubbing his head and the next he was back to typing again.

Grandpa Joe sat at his desk now and turned his chair to look at JJ, then he picked up the little plane and handed it to JJ.

'There you go, my boy, she's all yours.'

JJ was stunned. He had never even touched the plane before. It was almost an unspoken pact with his

Grandpa and Hannah that they didn't touch Flyer. He didn't know why but he felt it would somehow break Grandpa's connection with the plane. Now, however, he held it and smoothed it and turned it over and over in his hands, gazing at it in awe.

'But Grandpa Joe, the book,' he said.

'It's done, buddy! I sent it off yesterday, so I won't be needing her anymore. But take good care of her. She's meant an awful lot to me,' Grandpa Joe said, smiling and realizing that they would need to get a little something for Hannah too.

'I promise I'll take care of her forever and ever. I love her, Grandpa Joe,' JJ said. Grandpa knew that the time was now. He leaned forward and rested his elbows on his knees.

'Now hear me out, JJ. I want you to keep that plane where you can see it. I want you to let her remind you of the Wright Brothers. How against all the odds, they refused to quit, refused to give up their dream and fought until they succeeded. Can you imagine how many disappointments they must have gone through before they were able to achieve their goal?' Grandpa asked.

'I guess so,' JJ said, still looking in wonder at the little plane. `

'Now listen, all I've heard since you got back is how you never got to ride that roller coaster. I get it, JJ, I was small once you know, and now look at me.'

'I'm sorry, Grandpa,' JJ said, hanging his head.

'Hey,' Grandpa said, gently cupping and lifting JJ's chin. 'You don't ever need to apologize for expressing your disappointments to me. I wasn't criticizing you, I was merely pointing it out. No one gets it more than your family how disappointed you must be,' Grandpa said.

'Yeah, but nothing compares to Big Bend.' JJ hung his head again, trying to fight back yet more tears.

'Well, maybe not, but do you know what, you can always look forward to riding that another time. Imagine if the Wright Brothers had given up when their first attempt failed. Imagine if they had listened to all those folk who said they'd never do it. They knew in their hearts they would get there. They just had to believe. You won't always be this size, JJ, and no amount of worrying about it is gonna make you grow any quicker.'

'Yeah, but school, Damon and all those guys ...' JJ tailed off, he didn't need to spell it out.

'I know, I get how bullies work, remember what Jackson and I have been sayin'. Don't give them any more ammunition.

Look them in the eye and smile, JJ, tell them it's none of their business.'

'But, what if they push it?' JJ asked.

'Walk away, ask to use the bathroom. Go find Jerry or Hannah, just try not to get into it and if they push I want you to close your eyes real tight and picture me there. It worked before, it can work again.'

'But ...' Again words failed JJ.

'JJ, your Pa and Bernadette told us all about the other boys you met at the campsite. How old did you say they were? I think you said a couple were seventeen. Well let me tell you, that takes a mighty lot of guts and courage to hang out with them. You must have felt nervous at first,' Grandpa Joe said proudly.

'Yeah,' smiled JJ. 'They were pretty cool.'

'So how about we focus on them? How about you tell me how you got to talking with them and how that made you feel?'

JJ then proceeded to tell his Grandpa all about saving the tire swing and how he had been about to walk off when Chuck had called him back. How even when he had been too nervous to show up at the swing the following day, Chuck had come and found him. Chuck had gone out of his way to walk around the RV park, looking for JJ. JJ recounted that last night and all the funny stories around the campfire. His whole face lit up as he recounted the story and told Grandpa Joe how much he'd have loved it.

'You're right about that, my boy. I sure would have enjoyed that. So, with all these wonderful memories in mind, how about we forget Big Bend for now? How about we park him over there, under the paperweight? Maybe we can look at him again next year and for now let's talk about the rides you did get to go on at the first park; they must have been amazing?' Grandpa Joe asked.

'Some WERE pretty scary!' JJ admitted.

'Exactly, I bet they were and you know what? You DID it! You measured up for each and every other ride. You measured up to those bigger boys. You've measured up as an exceptional friend to young Jerry. Jackson tells me they struggled to catch Scarlett O'Hara last Saturday. He thinks she was protesting 'cuz you didn't go see her, so looks like you measure up at the ranch too! And then there's Toby. That silly mutt's been pining for you all week. He's been following us around and crying outside your room, so Grandma May's

been feeding him way too much – but you know how soft she is.'

'*I did miss him,'* JJ said smiling. He felt a lot lighter and Grandpa Joe was making a lot of sense.

'*So, you didn't get to ride Big Bend. You don't get picked for little league and yeah, I know, it hurts, but JJ, when you look at the bigger picture, you actually measure up a lot. You need to work on that strength. What happens if we don't water the crops?'* Grandpa asked.

'*They die,'* JJ answered.

'*Sure! We all need a little regular watering all the time. And lookin' after ourselves is not so different to crops or rearing a horse or a pup. You need to remember all you get right and stop beatin' yourself up when things go wrong.'*

'*Yeah, I guess I could try harder to work on that stuff,'* JJ said with a little more optimism.

'*Sure you can. And think about this; when Toby makes a mess inside, do you beat him?'*

'*No!'* JJ said appalled.

'*That's right, course you don't, and when the stupid mutt gets something right what do you do?'* Grandpa reasoned.

'*I give him a reward,'* JJ said.

'You know, JJ, you have choices and I'm not sayin' they're gonna be easy, but think of the Wright Brothers and Jerry. By choosing the right way of thinking about things, having the right attitude, we can fly. Have the wrong attitude, we'll 'crash and burn'. JJ, there will always be people who criticize, but no matter how many times we're knocked down, we can learn to get up again. We can learn to soar to greater heights just like the Wright Brothers!'

'Yeah, just like Flyer,' JJ said smiling at his new, most treasured possession.

'That's right! And then there's Jerry who doesn't let his disability hold him back but chooses to concentrate on his abilities. You see, JJ, what we believe affects how we behave, and ultimately what we become. Like Jerry you can choose to become a winner who sometimes loses – or be a loser who occasionally wins. Its your choice.'

'Yeah, Jerry's so cool,' JJ said, realizing that he couldn't wait to see his friend the following day for dinner, he had so much to tell him.

'OK, give me a few minutes; I promised your Grandma I would lift the turkey out the oven at five. I will be back with some more lemonade. I suppose I'd better let that mutt come too.'

After Grandpa left, JJ sat and stared around World HQ. He never felt bigger, stronger and safer than when he was here. This was home. This was his idea of heaven. Grandpa had made JJ see his life in a completely different light.

He thought of Jerry again. Jerry would never know what it was like to ride a roller coaster and yet he never complained. JJ smiled now as he pictured his best friend's face, lighting up as he whizzed down the ramp at school.

Jerry had an amazing outlook on life. Even though his disability could have easily held him back, he managed to soar in life while still being confined to a wheelchair.

JJ tingled as he stared at Old Faithful. What other masterpieces would emerge from that old machine, he wondered.

In that moment JJ realized his whole life was changing and it was all because of Grandpa Joe. The love he felt for his Grandpa knocked him sideways, it was bigger and stronger than anything he had ever encountered.

Grandpa Joe was the genius that encouraged JJ to

write. If he hadn't written in his notebook then Bernadette would never have found out just how unhappy JJ was and all the massive changes at home would not have taken place.

Grandpa had started out taking JJ to the ranch to hang out with Jackson for a couple of hours; now it had stretched to spending almost the entire weekend at the ranch. In the short time JJ had spent with her, Scarlett O'Hara had blossomed from a stroppy disinterested mare into a new horse that burst into life as soon as she saw him. Having her very own human come and care for her each week caused her to thrive.

And again – Jerry! When Damon had told Jerry that he would never get to ride Big Bend he had merely shrugged his shoulders and said: *'Yeah, but look at all I can do'* and then had spun his wheelchair around and around until he made himself dizzy.

Grandpa Joe returned, as promised, with two glasses of lemonade and Toby at his heels.

The two of them drank for a few moments in silence and with the overwhelming love in his heart. JJ felt he needed to say something.

'Hey, Grandpa Joe.' He choked on the words. Grandpa

came down, elbows to knees again.

'What is it, my boy?' he asked, concerned by the tears.

'I, I, I just gotta thank you for it all, for Pa and Bernadette, for makin' me write it down. I, it's all 'cuz of you that I...' Enough said. Grandpa got up and pulled JJ into his all embracing hug.

'You did it, not me,' Grandpa said. Confused JJ looked up into his Grandpa's eyes.

'What did I do? I did nothing,' he argued.

'Nonsense, you've heard the sayin' "you can lead a horse to water, but you can't make him drink."' Grandpa said smiling.

'I don't get it,' JJ said.

'Well, you can make it easy and show someone how to do something, but you can't force them to do it. You did the hard work, you made the right choices.'

'Right, we'd better scoot indoors before Grandma May gets cross and gives our dinner to Toby 'cuz he sure doesn't need anymore fattenin' up, I mean look at him,' Grandpa suggested.

Toby looked up on hearing his name, his little tail wagging frantically, his head looking tiny against his barrel tummy. Poor Toby, if he knew that Bernadette would soon have him on a strict diet once he got back to the farm he would sink into the depths of despair.

JJ picked up Flyer and held the little plane close to his chest.

'*This is the best gift in the whole wide world, Grandpa,*' he said.

As they left World HQ, they could just about make out a passenger jet flying high above them. It would have been almost invisible except for the white streak of vapor trail it left behind. JJ and Grandpa Joe stopped and watched as the plane flew off in the clear Texas sky. Then it was gone and all that was left were the white tracks of its journey still magically painted in the clear blue sky.

'I wonder what the Wright Brothers would think about that! Bet they never thought their invention could turn into something like that, do you, Grandpa?' JJ asked.

'There's a big difference, that's for sure, but I'll bet they're both up there lookin' down here, and wishin' they would've had a chance to try it,' Grandpa responded.

'Grandpa Joe, do you think that they would have liked jet planes? Or do you think they would say that they could have invented something better?' JJ asked.

'I think they would have been proud to be the beginning of something way beyond their imagination. They changed aviation history. You could even say they changed the world!'

'Huh!' JJ thought, 'I guess it doesn't matter what OTHER PEOPLE think of you. It's what you think about YOURSELF that counts. I mean, **"How tall do you have to be to change the world?"'**

THE END

ABOUT THE AUTHORS

Chris Spicer is a leader with over fifty years experience working with Christian communities and learning centers throughout Europe and North America. Having lived in Portland, Oregon and Peoria, Illinois, Chris now lives with his wife Tina in England – they have four adult children and eight rock-star grandchildren.

Catherine Lawless is an author and songwriter who has written under a pseudonym on the subject of domestic abuse. She is married and a mother to a teenage daughter and lives in Hertfordshire, England.

Let's Go Round Again!

COMPLEMENTARY LEARNING RESOURCE

AVAILABLE FOR DOWNLOAD

www.mediafire.com/file/fc1t76rhkwa8t1z/

ComplementaryLearningResource.pdf/file